HOME TO HARLEM

Home to Harlem

by CLAUDE McKAY

Foreword by

WAYNE F. COOPER

NORTHEASTERN UNIVERSITY PRESS
Boston
Published by University Press of New England
Hanover and London

NORTHEASTERN UNIVERSITY PRESS

Published by University Press of New England,
One Court Street, Lebanon, NH 03766
www.upne.com

First published in 1928 by Harper & Brothers
First Northeastern University Press edition 1987

Printed in the United States of America
15

ISBN-13: 978-1-55553-024-2
ISBN-10: 1-55553-024-9

Library of Congress Cataloging-in-Publication Data
McKay, Claude, 1890–1948
Home to Harlem.
Reprint. Originally published: New York : Harper, 1928.
With new foreword.
I. Title.
PS3525.A24785H6   1987   813'.52   87–15357
ISBN 1-55553-023-0 (alk. paper)
ISBN 1-55553-024-9 (pbk.: alk. paper)

TO MY FRIEND
LOUISE BRYANT

CONTENTS

FOREWORD TO THE 1987 EDITION

*O*F all the major Afro-American writers who emerged in the 1920s, Claude McKay remains the most controversial and least understood. Those among the general public who recognize his name at all will recall him as the author of "If We Must Die," a defiant sonnet of black resistance before mob violence. A few may also remember him as the author of *Home to Harlem,* the first and best-known work of his four volumes of fiction published between 1928 and 1933. It has often been called the first Afro-American "best seller," because of the brief vogue it enjoyed in New York City before the stock market crash of 1929 and the Great Depression sent black writers and their literature into deep eclipse. Not until the publication of Richard Wright's *Native Son* in 1940 did another Afro-American novel enjoy such popular success.

Before writing *Home to Harlem,* McKay had already established himself as a poet. Born in the mountains of central Jamaica in 1890 of black peasant parents, McKay published two volumes of Jamaican dialect poetry, *Songs of Jamaica* (1912) and *Constab Ballads* (1912), before he left for the United States in 1912. Once in the United States, McKay abandoned dialect verse and, instead, began to write sonnets. He also continued to move politically to the left. Just after World War I, McKay emerged in New York City as a militant Communist poet. He joined Max and Crystal Eastman on the revolutionary arts journal the *Liberator* (the successor to the more famous *Masses*). In the poetry he wrote for the *Liberator* between 1919 and 1922, he expressed the alienation, anger, and rebellion Afro-Americans experienced in the face of racial prejudice. During these years, McKay also wrote love sonnets and lyrics evocative of a lost pastoral childhood in Jamaica.

In 1920, he spent a year in England working as a journalist on Sylvia Pankhurst's weekly, *Worker's Dreadnought*. While there, he also published a slim volume of his new verse, *Spring in New Hampshire* (1920). Returning to New York City in 1921, he became a co-editor of the *Liberator*. In 1922, he published *Harlem Shadows,* which included the best of his militant sonnets since 1912.

While on the *Liberator,* McKay had attacked the extreme conservatism of most black critics who often viewed black art simply as an extension of racial uplift efforts. As a result, McKay believed, they tended to stifle the kind of free expression in literature and drama that was already making popular Afro-American music a vital and universally appreciated medium. Against such freer forms of Afro-American popular expression, black critics held up as models those black artists who achieved excellence in the classic forms of Western music, art, and literature. As McKay wrote in his review for the *Liberator* of the Afro-American musical *Shuffle Along:*

The Negro critics can scarcely perceive
and recognize true values through the
screen of sneering bigotry put between
them and life by the dominant race. . . .
Negro art, these critics declare, must be
dignified and respectable like the Anglo-
Saxon's before it can be good. The Negro
must get the warmth, color and laughter
out of his blood, else the white man will
sneer at him and treat him with contumely.
Happily the Negro retains his joy of living
in the teeth of such criticism; and in Harlem, along Fifth and Lenox avenues, in
Marcus Garvey's Hall with its extravagant
paraphernalia, in his churches and cabarets, he expresses himself with a zest that
is yet to be depicted by a true artist.[1]

In New York and in London, McKay became
aware of the growing appreciation of African
art, Afro-American jazz, and other forms of

---

1. Claude McKay, review of *Shuffle Along, Liberator*, Vol. 4 (Decem-
ber, 1921): 24–26.

Afro-American music among white critics and white artists. In *The Negroes in America,* he declared that "our age is the age of Negro art. The slogan of the aesthetic art world is 'Return to the Primitive.' The Futurists and Impressionists are agreed in turning everything upside-down in an attempt to achieve the wisdom of the primitive Negro" (p. 63). In the same work, McKay also expressed an appreciation of the growing importance in America and elsewhere of ethnic literatures that concentrated on the specific characteristics and experiences of particular minorities; he cited as his chief example the growth of Jewish-American literature.

Finally, McKay was strongly influenced by contemporary novelists Sherwood Anderson and D. H. Lawrence. He considered Lawrence, in particular, a spiritual brother, though they never met. With writers like Anderson and Lawrence, he shared a deep faith in the primitive life forces in human nature, as opposed to the artificial constraints imposed upon humanity by modern industrial society. In particular,

McKay believed that Afro-Americans, especially the rural Afro-Americans of Jamaica and the American South, were closer to the earth and more natural in their responses to life than the white urban population of over-industrialized Europe and America.

In his American verses (and earlier, in his Jamaican dialect poetry), McKay expressed with great clarity and vigor his race's deepest emotions as an alienated, besieged, and tormented minority within Western civilization. At the same time, he also proclaimed himself a universalist, a Communist internationalist, and a free spirit. In 1922, he traveled to the Soviet Union. While there, he wrote an account of American race relations and outlined a program for Afro-American assimilation into the American Communist movement. His account was published in Moscow as *The Negroes in America* (1923, 1979). In Russia, too, he published his first volume of fiction, a slim pamphlet of short stories entitled *Trial by Lynching* (1925, 1977). These stories were hurriedly written and much more overtly propagandistic than his later fiction.

After deciding in Russia that he must not subordinate his freedom as a literary artist to the emerging Soviet-dominated, Communist International political orthodoxy, McKay arrived in France in 1923 determined to earn his way as a novelist. To H. L. Mencken, he wrote that he planned "to do a series of prose sketches of my contacts in America, using the most significant things, yet, leaving no subject, however degraded, untouched. Much of the period 1914–1919 was spent in the so-called semi-underworld and should make interesting reading from the point of view I shall write from. I have the whole thing planned in my head and I see the scenes in a finer perspective from here."[2]

For the next five years, McKay struggled to master prose fiction. With the friendly support, advice, and encouragement of Louise Bryant

2. Claude McKay, quoted in Wayne F. Cooper, *Claude McKay: Rebel Sojourner in the Harlem Renaissance, A Life* (Baton Rouge: Louisiana State University Press, 1987): 212.

Bullitt and Sinclair Lewis, he managed to complete one novel, "Color Scheme," by the fall of 1925. To a friend in the United States, he wrote that the leadership of the National Association for the Advancement of Colored People might find "Color Scheme" shocking, even immoral. He described it as a satire in "black and white" that ignored the genteel traditions that had previously constrained earlier black novelists. "I make my Negro characters yarn and backbite and fuck like people the world over," he exclaimed.[3]

American publishers found "Color Scheme" uneven in quality and much too explicit in its sexual frankness and language to be published. In anger and despair, McKay burned the novel and wrote a series of short stories, which Louise Bryant Bullitt submitted to Harper and Brothers in the fall of 1926. She also urged McKay to allow an American literary agent in Paris, William Aspenwall Bradley, to represent him. Brad-

3. Ibid., 217–218.

ley secured for McKay a long-term contract with Harper, which urged him to expand one of his short stories, "Home to Harlem" into a novel. McKay eagerly complied and *Home to Harlem* appeared in 1928 at the height of the New Negro or Harlem Renaissance period.

While McKay remained abroad, a younger generation of black writers had begun to break the restraints of the genteel protest tradition prescribed by an older Afro-American leadership. Langston Hughes, Jean Toomer, Rudolph Fisher, Zora Neale Hurston, and Nella Larsen had begun to expand the boundaries of Afro-American literature in the face of conservative Afro-American criticism. At the same time, a Negro vogue among New York critics had begun to make Harlem cabarets and night spots and Afro-American music and literature increasingly attractive to the literate white public, especially in New York City.

By its vividness and by its explicit depiction of the seamier sides of Harlem's growing population of working-class blacks, *Home to Harlem* sparked even more critical commentary. It quickly reaped both exaggerated praise and condemnation. Conservative black critics condemned it as a strictly commercial work that pandered to the worst stereotypes of Afro-Americans held by white America, while some white reviewers praised it uncritically as "the real thing in rightness . . . the lowdown on Harlem, the dope from the inside."[4] Black critics such as W. E. B. DuBois in *Crisis* and Dewey Jones in the Chicago *Defender* protested such uncritical acceptance. After reading *Home to Harlem,* DuBois remarked that he had felt unclean and in need of a bath. Jones bemoaned the fact that "white people think we are buffoons, thugs, and rotters anyway. Why should we waste so much time trying to prove it? That's what Claude McKay has done."[5]

To the youthful Langston Hughes, who had already begun to battle for greater Afro-American literary freedom in America, *Home to*

4. Ibid, 245.
5. Ibid.

Harlem was a welcome addition and McKay a welcome ally in the fight. To McKay, he declared that "undoubtedly it is the finest thing 'we've' done yet. . . . Your novel ought to give a second youth to the Negro Vogue."[6] After five years of struggle, *Home to Harlem*'s popular success gave McKay great satisfaction. In April, 1928, McKay noted to William Aspenwall Bradley with satisfaction that "I see *Home to Harlem* like an impudent dog has [moved] right in among the best-sellers in New York."[7] To others, McKay wrote that he understood but did not agree with his black critics' objections to his frank exploitation of "low-class Negro life. We must," he concluded in one letter, "leave the appreciation of what we are doing to the emancipated Negro intelligentsia of the future, while we are sardonically aware now that only the intelligentsia of the superior race is developed enough to afford artistic truth."[8] To the black

6. Ibid, 243.
7. Ibid, 237.
8. Ibid, 247.

journalist J. A. Rogers, he further remarked that "it will take the Negro in America another thirty or forty years to see *Home to Harlem* in its true light—to appreciate it in the spirit in which I wrote it."[9]

Today, as never before, *Home to Harlem* deserves a fresh reading. The issues it examined and the portrait it drew of Harlem in the 1920s foreshadowed both the vast problems and the vast potentials locked within that portion of the Afro-American population that has remained restricted, impoverished, congested, and only marginally employed by American corporate society.

In writing *Home to Harlem,* McKay consciously attempted to portray what he described as "the semi-underworld" of single, black, working-class men in the industrial Northeast in the years just after World War I. They were all migrants from the American South or the West Indies, with whom he worked and fraternized in

9. Ibid.

New York City between 1914 and 1919. McKay describes their work, their play, and their relationships with women, each other, and their community.

Within the larger Harlem community, as within American society, McKay's characters in *Home to Harlem* occupied a marginal position. They were largely uneducated. They lived in boarding houses and in what today might be called "single-room occupancy" hotels. Their love affairs tended to be brief and fraught with ambivalence; they often ended abruptly, sometimes violently. The women with whom they became involved had their own incomes as cooks, domestics, entertainers, waitresses, or clerks; some worked as part time prostitutes. Between the men and women in *Home to Harlem*, there existed both passionate tenderness and competitiveness, a mutually jealous independence of spirit that often resulted in antagonism and separation.

Their places of entertainment were cabarets, night clubs, saloons, pool halls, gambling dens, buffet flats, and houses of prostitution. They imbibed alcohol freely; some sniffed cocaine or smoked opium. They lived with a potential for violence emanating from white society and from their own desperate desire for a freer life. Self-hatred, color-complexes, sexual struggle, corruption, drug addiction, ghetto congestion, and class divisions within Afro-America can be found in *Home to Harlem*. McKay was aware of these problems, and he neither ignored nor apologized for them as simply the consequences of the white injustices committed against Afro-America.

In *Home to Harlem*, as in all his fiction, McKay chose to demonstrate that despite all the horrors visited upon Afro-Americans by white oppression, there existed among even the least privileged Afro-Americans a healthy determination to live and to enjoy the fruits of life. It is this passionate embrace of life that sometimes justified in their minds the negative aspects of their existence. When the novel's hero, Jake Brown, tells his fellow black longshoremen that it is wrong to cross picket lines and work as "scabs," one black man angrily retorts that black workers were often shut out of union jobs and asserts that Jake was "talking death, tha's what you sure is. One thing I know is niggers am made foh life. And I want to live, boh, and feel plenty o' the juice o' life in mah blood. I wanta live and I wanta love. And niggers am got to work hard foh that. Buddy, I'll tell you this and I'll tell it to the wo'l'—all the crackers, and all them poah white trash, all the nigger-hitting and nigger-breaking white folks—I loves life and I got to live and I'll scab through hell to live."

Jake listens but demurs; he is Claude McKay's symbol of primitive Afro-American decency and vitality. It is Jake's picaresque journey through "the semi-underworld" of black working-class America that we follow in *Home to Harlem*. After he joins the Pennsylvania Railroad as a third cook in their dining-car service, he meets the waiter, Ray, a displaced Haitian intellectual. A friendship develops that allows McKay to complement and contrast their respective

strengths and weaknesses against a background
of rough-and-tumble work and night life.

It is a life that is entirely black, and despite its
severe limitations (which both Jake and Ray
recognize), it achieves certain positive expressions that emerge most clearly in the music,
dance, and laughter of black men and women
together at night. They are lost in enjoyment of
themselves, revealing their own hard-won crea-
tivity, color, and joy in life: "Black lovers of life
caught up in their own free native rhythm,
threaded to a remote scarce-remembered past,
celebrating the midnight hours in themselves,
for themselves, of themselves, in a house in
Fifteenth Street, Philadelphia. . . ." Against
such lyrical aspects of Afro-American life as
McKay himself had, in fact, experienced as a
dining-car waiter on the Pennsylvania Railroad
during World War I, there is also in *Home to
Harlem* a less optimistic recognition that Afro-
American life in Harlem and in other developing
Northeast ghettoes was too confined and congested. Frustration and self-hatred often result-

ed from such conditions, and self-inflicted violence was a constant threat to everyone in the community. In *Home to Harlem,* McKay celebrated the potential of the Afro-American community but remained aware of the pressures within it that threatened its future.

With *Home to Harlem,* McKay began a fictional search for value, meaning, and self-direction in modern Afro-American existence that would preoccupy him in future works.[10] Despite all the brave assertions of Afro-American vitality and joy in the novel, it was a troubled book by an author whose own tensions and doubts were never far from the surface. Nevertheless, McKay's portraits of Jake and Ray were positive ones. Threads of affirmation and hope pervade their story that, with few exceptions, have remained constant in black fiction, despite the enormity of the problems that still beset America's black inner cities

10. *Banjo* (1929), *Gingertown* (1932), *Banana Bottom* (1933), *A Long Way From Home* (1937), and *Harlem, Negro Metropolis* (1940).

today. McKay believed that the black folk wisdom brought to the nation's cities in the Great Migration northward that began in his day was exemplified in men like Jake in *Home to Harlem*. These men possessed both a hard realism and a generosity of spirit upon which the black community had to build if it were ever to take control of its own destiny and cease to be the victim of heedless American capitalism that viewed Afro-Americans as inert pawns upon a chessboard of profit and loss.

July 1987   W.F.C.

FIRST PART

GOING BACK HOME

I

*A*LL that Jake knew about the freighter on which he stoked was that it stank between sea and sky. He was working with a dirty Arab crew. The captain signed him on at Cardiff because one of the Arabs had quit the ship. Jake was used to all sorts of rough jobs, but he had never before worked in such a filthy dinghy.

The white sailors who washed the ship would not wash the stokers' water-closet, because they despised the Arabs. And the Arabs themselves made no effort to keep the place clean, although it adjoined their sleeping berth.

The cooks hated the Arabs because they did not eat pork. Whenever there was pork for dinner, something else had to be prepared for the Arabs. The cooks put the stokers' meat, cut in unappetizing chunks, in a broad pan, and the two kinds of vegetables in two other pans. The stoker who carried the food back to the bunks always put one pan inside of the other, and sometimes the bottoms were dirty and bits of potato peelings or egg shells were mixed in with the meat and the vegetables.

The Arabs took up a chunk of meat with their coal-powdered fingers, bit or tore off a piece, and tossed the chunk back into the pan. It was strange to Jake that these Arabs washed themselves after eating and not before. They ate with their clothes stiff-starched to their bodies with coal and sweat. And when they were finished, they stripped and washed and went to sleep in the stinking-dirty bunks. Jake was used to the lowest and hardest sort of life, but even his leather-lined stomach could not endure the Arabs' way of eating. Jake also began to despise the Arabs. He complained to the cooks about the food. He gave the chef a ten-shilling note, and the chef gave him his eats separately.

One of the sailors flattered Jake. "You're

the same like us chaps. You ain't like them
dirty jabbering coolies."

But Jake smiled and shook his head in a
non-committal way. He knew that if he was
just like the white sailors, he might have
signed on as a deckhand and not as a stoker.
He didn't care about the dirty old boat, anyhow. It was taking him back home—that was
all he cared about. He made his shift all
right, stoking four hours and resting eight.
He didn't sleep well. The stokers' bunks were
lousy, and fetid with the mingled smell of stale
food and water-closet. Jake had attempted to
keep the place clean, but to do that was impossible. Apparently the Arabs thought that
a sleeping quarters could also serve as a
garbage can.

"Nip me all you wanta, Mister Louse," said
Jake. "Roll on, Mister Ship, and stinks all
the way as you rolls. Jest take me 'long to
Harlem is all I pray. I'm crazy to see again
the brown-skin chippies 'long Lenox Avenue.
Oh boy!"

Jake was tall, brawny, and black. When

[3]

America declared war upon Germany in 1917
he was a longshoreman. He was working on
a Brooklyn pier, with a score of men under
him. He was a little boss and a very good
friend of his big boss, who was Irish. Jake
thought he would like to have a crack at the
Germans. . . . And he enlisted.

In the winter he sailed for Brest with a
happy chocolate company. Jake had his own
daydreams of going over the top. But his
company was held at Brest. Jake toted
lumber—boards, planks, posts, rafters—for the
hundreds of huts that were built around the
walls of Brest and along the coast between
Brest and Saint-Pierre, to house the United
States soldiers.

Jake was disappointed. He had enlisted to
fight. For what else had he been sticking a
bayonet into the guts of a stuffed man and aim-
ing bullets straight into a bull's-eye? Toting
planks and getting into rows with his white
comrades at the Bal Musette were not ad-
venture.

Jake obtained leave. He put on civilian

[4]

clothes and lit out for Havre. He liquored himself up and hung round a low-down café in Havre for a week.

One day an English sailor from a Channel sloop made up to Jake. "Darky," he said, "you 'arvin' a good time 'round 'ere."

Jake thought how strange it was to hear the Englishman say "darky" without being offended. Back home he would have been spoiling for a fight. There he would rather hear "nigger" than "darky," for he knew that when a Yankee said "nigger" he meant hatred for Negroes, whereas when he said "darky" he meant friendly contempt. He preferred white folks' hatred to their friendly contempt. To feel their hatred made him strong and aggressive, while their friendly contempt made him ridiculously angry, even against his own will.

"Sure Ise having a good time, all right," said Jake. He was making a cigarette and growling cusses at French tobacco. "But Ise got to get a move on 'fore very long."

"Where to?" his new companion asked.

"Any place, Buddy. I'm always ready for something new," announced Jake.

"Been in Havre a long time?"

"Week or two," said Jake. "I tooks care of some mules over heah. Twenty, God damn them, days across the pond. And then the boat plows round and run off and leaves me behind. Kain you beat that, Buddy?"

"It wasn't the best o' luck," replied the other. "Ever been to London?"

"Nope, Buddy," said Jake. "France is the only country I've struck yet this side the water."

The Englishman told Jake that there was a sailor wanted on his tug.

"We never 'ave a full crew—since the war," he said.

Jake crossed over to London. He found plenty of work there as a docker. He liked the West India Docks. He liked Limehouse. In the pubs men gave him their friendly paws and called him "darky." He liked how they called him "darky." He made friends. He

found a woman. He was happy in the East
End.

The Armistice found him there. On New-
Year's Eve, 1919, Jake went to a monster
dance with his woman, and his docker friends
and their women, in the Mile End Road.

The Armistice had brought many more
black men to the East End of London. Hundreds of them. Some of them found work.
Some did not. Many were getting a little
pension from the government. The price of
sex went up in the East End, and the dignity
of it also. And that summer Jake saw a big
battle staged between the colored and white
men of London's East End. Fisticuffs, razor
and knife and gun play. For three days his
woman would not let him out-of-doors. And
when it was all over he was seized with the
awful fever of lonesomeness. He felt all alone
in the world. He wanted to run away from
the kind-heartedness of his lady of the East
End.

"Why did I ever enlist and come over
here?" he asked himself. "Why did I want

to mix mahself up in a white folks' war? It ain't ever was any of black folks' affair. Niggers am evah always such fools, anyhow. Always thinking they've got something to do with white folks' business."

Jake's woman could do nothing to please him now. She tried hard to get down into his thoughts and share them with him. But for Jake this woman was now only a creature of another race—of another world. He brooded day and night.

It was two years since he had left Harlem. Fifth Avenue, Lenox Avenue, and One Hundred and Thirty-fifth Street, with their chocolate-brown and walnut-brown girls, were calling him.

"Oh, them legs!" Jake thought. "Them tantalizing brown legs! . . . Barron's Cabaret! . . . Leroy's Cabaret! . . . Oh, boy!"

Brown girls rouged and painted like dark pansies. Brown flesh draped in soft colorful clothes. Brown lips full and pouted for sweet kissing. Brown breasts throbbing with love.

"Harlem for mine!" cried Jake. "I was

[8]

crazy thinkin' I was happy over heah. I wasn't mahself. I was like a man charged up with dope every day. That's what it was. Oh, boy! Harlem for mine!

"Take me home to Harlem, Mister Ship! Take me home to the brown gals waiting for the brown boys that done show their mettle over there. Take me home, Mister Ship. Put your beak right into that water and jest move along." . . .

ARRIVAL

II

*J*AKE was paid off. He changed a pound note he had brought with him. He had fifty-nine dollars. From South Ferry he took an express subway train for Harlem.

Jake drank three Martini cocktails with cherries in them. The price, he noticed, had gone up from ten to twenty-five cents. He went to Bank's and had a Maryland fried-chicken feed—a big one with candied sweet potatoes.

He left his suitcase behind the counter of a saloon on Lenox Avenue. He went for a promenade on Seventh Avenue between One Hundred and Thirty-fifth and One Hundred and Fortieth Streets. He thrilled to Harlem. His blood was hot. His eyes were alert as he sniffed the street like a hound. Seventh Avenue was nice, a little too nice that night.

Jake turned off on Lenox Avenue. He

stopped before an ice-cream parlor to admire girls sipping ice-cream soda through straws. He went into a cabaret. . . .

A little brown girl aimed the arrow of her eye at him as he entered. Jake was wearing a steel-gray English suit. It fitted him loosely and well, perfectly suited his presence. She knew at once that Jake must have just landed. She rested her chin on the back of her hands and smiled at him. There was something in his attitude, in his hungry wolf's eyes, that went warmly to her. She was brown, but she had tinted her leaf-like face to a ravishing chestnut. She had on an orange scarf over a green frock, which was way above her knees, giving an adequate view of legs lovely in fine champagne-colored stockings. . . .

Her shaft hit home. . . . Jake crossed over to her table. He ordered Scotch and soda.

"Scotch is better with soda or even water," he said. "English folks don't take whisky straight, as we do."

But she preferred ginger ale in place of soda. The cabaret singer, seeing that they were making up to each other, came expressly over to their table and sang. Jake gave the singer fifty cents. . . .

Her left hand was on the table. Jake covered it with his right.

"Is it clear sailing between us, sweetie?" he asked.

"Sure thing. . . . You just landed from over there?"

"Just today!"

"But there wasn't no boat in with soldiers today, daddy."

"I made it in a special one."

"Why, you lucky baby! . . . I'd like to go to another place, though. What about you?"

"Anything you say, I'm game," responded Jake.

They walked along Lenox Avenue. He held her arm. His flesh tingled. He felt as if his whole body was a flaming wave. She was intoxicated, blinded under the overwhelming force.

But nevertheless she did not forget her business.

"How much is it going to be, daddy?" she demanded.

"How much? *How* much? Five?"

"Aw no, daddy. . . ."

"Ten?"

She shook her head.

"Twenty, sweetie!" he said, gallantly.

"Daddy," she answered, "I wants fifty."

"Good," he agreed. He was satisfied. She was responsive. She was beautiful. He loved the curious color on her cheek.

They went to a buffet flat on One Hundred and Thirty-seventh Street. The proprietress opened the door without removing the chain and peeked out. She was a matronly mulatto woman. She recognized the girl, who had put herself in front of Jake, and she slid back the chain and said, "Come right in."

The windows were heavily and carefully shaded. There was beer and wine, and there was plenty of hard liquor. Black and brown men sat at two tables in one room, playing

[13]

poker. In the other room a phonograph was grinding out a "blues," and some couples were dancing, thick as maggots in a vat of sweet liquor, and as wriggling.

Jake danced with the girl. They shuffled warmly, gloriously about the room. He encircled her waist with both hands, and she put both of hers up to his shoulders and laid her head against his breast. And they shuffled around.

"Harlem! Harlem!" thought Jake. "Where else could I have all this life but Harlem? Good old Harlem! Chocolate Harlem! Sweet Harlem! Harlem, I've got you' number down. Lenox Avenue, you're a bear, I know it. And, baby honey, sure enough youse a pippin for your pappy. Oh, boy!" . . .

After Jake had paid for his drinks, that fifty-dollar note was all he had left in the world. He gave it to the girl. . . .

"Is we going now, honey?" he asked her.

"Sure, daddy. Let's beat it." . . .

Oh, to be in Harlem again after two years away. The deep-dyed color, the thickness, the closeness of it. The noises of Harlem. The sugared laughter. The honey-talk on its streets. And all night long, ragtime and "blues" p l a y i n g somewhere, . . . singing somewhere, dancing somewhere! Oh, the contagious fever of Harlem. Burning everywhere in dark-eyed Harlem. . . . Burning now in Jake's sweet blood. . . .

He woke up in the morning in a state of perfect peace. She brought him hot coffee and cream and doughnuts. He yawned. He sighed. He was satisfied. He breakfasted. He washed. He dressed. The sun was shining. He sniffed the fine dry air. Happy, familiar Harlem.

"I ain't got a cent to my name," mused Jake, "but ahm as happy as a prince, all the same. Yes, I is."

He loitered down Lenox Avenue. He shoved his hand in his pocket—pulled out the fifty-dollar note. A piece of paper was pinned to it on which was scrawled in pencil:

"Just a little gift from a baby girl to a honey boy!"

ZEDDY

III

"GREAT balls of fire! Looka here! See mah luck!" Jake stopped in his tracks . . . went on . . . stopped again . . . retraced his steps . . . checked himself. "Guess I won't go back right now. Never let a woman think you're too crazy about her. But she's a particularly sweet piece a business. . . . Me and her again tonight. . . . Handful o' luck shot straight outa heaven. Oh, boy! Harlem is mine!"

Jake went rolling along Fifth Avenue. He crossed over to Lenox Avenue and went into Uncle Doc's saloon, where he had left his bag. Called for a glass of Scotch. "Gimme the siphon, Doc. I'm off the straight stuff."

"Iszh you? Counta what?"

"Hits the belly better this way. I l'arned it over the other side."

A slap on the shoulder brought him sharply

round. "Zeddy Plummer! What grave is you arisen from?" he cried.

"Buddy, you looks so good to me, I could kish you," Zeddy said.

"Where?"

"Everywhere. . . . French style."

"One on one cheek and one on the other."

"Savee-vous?"

"Parlee-vous?"

Uncle Doc set another glass on the counter and poured out pure Bourbon. Zeddy reached a little above Jake's shoulders. He was stocky, thick-shouldered, flat-footed, and walked like a bear. Some more customers came in and the buddies eased round to the short side of the bar.

"What part of the earth done belch you out?" demanded Zeddy. "Nevah heared no God's tidings a you sence we missed you from Brest."

"And how about you?" Jake countered. "Didn't them Germans git you scrambling over the top?"

"Nevah see'd them, buddy. None a them

showed the goose-step around Brest. Have a
shot on me. . . . Well, dawg bite me, but—
say, Jake, we've got some more stuff to booze
over."

Zeddy slapped Jake on his breast and
looked him over again. "Tha's some stuff
you're strutting in, boh. 'Tain't 'Merican and
it ain't French." . . .

"English." Jake showed his clean white
teeth.

"Mah granny an' me! You been in that
theah white folks' country, too?"

"And don't I look as if Ise been? Where
else could a fellow git such good and cheap
man clothes to cover his skin?"

"Buddy, I know it's the trute. What you
doing today?"

"No, when you make me think ovit, particular thing. And you?"

"I'm alongshore but—I ain't agwine to
work thisaday."

"I guess I've got to be heaving along right
back to it, too, in pretty short time. I got to
get me a room but——"

Uncle Doc reminded Jake that his suit-case was there.

"I ain't nevah fohgitting all mah worldly goods," responded Jake.

Zeddy took Jake to a pool-room where they played. Jake was the better man. From the pool-room they went to Aunt Hattie's chitterling joint in One Hundred and Thirty-second Street, where they fed. Fricassee chicken and rice. Green peas. Stewed corn.

Aunt Hattie's was renowned among the lowly of Harlem's Black Belt. It was a little basement joint, smoke-colored. And Aunt Hattie was weather-beaten dark-brown, cheery-faced, with two rusty-red front teeth sticking together conspicuously out of her twisted, spread-away mouth. She cooked delicious food—home-cooked food they called it. None of the boys loafing round that section of Fifth Avenue would dream of going to any other place for their "poke chops."

Aunt Hattie admired her new customer from the kitchen door and he quite filled her sight. And when she went with the dish rag to wipe the oil-cloth before setting down the cocoanut pie, she rubbed her breast against Jake's shoulder and a sensual light gleamed in her aged smoke-red eyes.

The buddies talked about the days of Brest. Zeddy recalled the everlasting unloading and unloading of ships and the toting of lumber. The house of the Young Men's Christian Association, overlooking the harbor, where colored soldiers were not wanted. . . . The central Rue de Siam and the point near the Prefecture of Marine, from which you could look down on the red lights of the Quartier Réservé. The fatal fights between black men and white in the *maisons closes*. The encounters between apaches and white Americans. The French sailors that couldn't get the Yankee idea of amour and men. And the cemetery, just beyond the old mediæval gate of the town, where he left his second-best buddy.

"Poor boh. Was always belly-aching for a chance over the top. Nevah got it nor nothing. Not even a baid in the hospital. Strong

like a bull, yet just knocked off in the dark
through raw cracker cussedness. . . . Some
life it was, buddy, in them days. We was always on the defensive as if the boches, as the
froggies called them, was right down on us."

"Yet you stuck t'rough it toting lumber.
Got back to Harlem all right, though."

"You bet I did, boh. You kain trust Zeddy
Plummer to look out for his own black hide.
. . . But you, buddy. How come you just
vanished thataway like a spook? How did
you take your tail out ovit?"

Jake told Zeddy how he walked out of it
straight to the station in Brest. Le Havre.
London. The West India Docks. And back
home to Harlem.

"But you must keep it dark, buddy," Zeddy
cautioned. "Don't go shooting off your mouth
too free. Gov'mant still smoking out deserters
and draft dodgers."

"I ain't told no nigger but you, boh. Nor
ofay, neither. Ahm in your confidence,
chappie."

"That's all right, buddy." Zeddy put his

hand on Jake's knee. "It's better to keep your business close all the time. But I'll tell you this for your perticular information. Niggers am awful close-mouthed in some things. There is fellows here in Harlem that just telled the draft to mount upstairs. Pohlice and soldiers were hunting ev'where foh them. And they was right here in Harlem. Fifty dollars apiece foh them. All their friends knowed it and not a one gived them in. I tell you, niggers am amazing sometimes. Yet other times, without any natural reason, they will just go vomiting out their guts to the ofays about one another."

"God; but it's good to get back home again!" said Jake.

"I should think you was hungry foh a li'l' brown honey. I tell you trute, buddy. I made mine ovah there, spitin' ov ev'thing. I l'arned her a little z'inglise and she l'arned me beaucoup plus the French stuff. . . . The real stuff, buddy. But I was tearin' mad and glad to get back all the same. Take it from me, buddy, there ain't no honey lak to that theah comes out of our own belonging-to-us honeycomb."

"Man, what you telling me?" cried Jake. "Don't I knows it? What else you think made me leave over the other side? And dog mah doggone ef I didn't find it just as I landed."

"K-hhhhhhh! K-hhhhhhhh!" Zeddy laughed. "Dog mah cats! You done tasted the real life a'ready?"

"Last night was the end of the world, buddy, and tonight ahm going back there," chanted Jake as he rose and began kicking up his heels round the joint.

Zeddy also got up and put on his gray cap. They went back to the pool-room. Jake met two more fellows that he knew and got into a ring of Zeddy's pals. . . . Most of them were longshoremen. There was plenty of work, Jake learned. Before he left the pool-room he and Zeddy agreed to meet the next evening at Uncle Doc's.

"Got to work tomorrow, boh," Zeddy informed Jake.

. . . .

"Good old New York! The same old wench of a city. Elevated racketing over you' head. Subway bellowing under you' feet. Me foh wrastling round them piers again. Scratching down to the bottom of them ships and scrambling out. All alongshore for me now. No more fooling with the sea. Same old New York. Everybody dashing round like crazy. . . . Same old New York. But the ofay faces am different from those ovah across the pond. Sure they is. Stiffer. Tighter. Yes, they is that. . . . But the sun does better here than over there. And the sky's so high and dry and blue. And the air it—O Gawd it works in you' flesh and blood like Scotch. O Lawdy, Lawdy! I wants to live to a hundred and finish mah days in New York."

Jake threw himself up as if to catch the air pouring down from the blue sky. . . .

"Harlem! Harlem! Little thicker, little darker and noisier and smellier, but Harlem just the same. The niggers done plowed through Hundred and Thirtieth Street.

[25]

Heading straight foh One Hundred and Twenty-fifth. Spades beyond Eighth Avenue. Going, going, going Harlem! Going up! Nevah befoh I seed so many dickty shines in sich swell motor-cars. Plenty moh nigger shops. Seventh Avenue done gone high-brown. O Lawdy! Harlem bigger, Harlem better . . . and sweeter."

. . . .

"Street and streets! One Hundred and Thirty-second, Thirty-third, Thirty-fourth. It wasn't One Hundred and Thirty-fifth and it wasn't beyond theah. . . . O Lawd! how did I fohgit to remember the street and number. I reeled outa there like a drunken man. I been so happy. . . .

"Thirty-f o u r t h, Thirty-second, Thirty-third. . . . Only difference in the name. All the streets am just the same and all the houses 'like as peas. I could try this one heah or that one there but —— Rabbit foot! I didn't even git her name. Oh, Jakie, Jake! What a big Ah-Ah you is.

"I was a fool not to go back right then when

I feeled like it. What did I want to tighten up mahself and crow and strut like a crazy cat for? A grand Ah-Ah I is. Feet in mah hands! Take me back to the Baltimore to-night. I ain't gwine to know no peace till I lay these here hands on mah tantalizing brown again."

CONGO ROSE

IV

*A*LL the old cabarets were going still. Connor's was losing ground. The bed of red roses that used to glow in the ceiling was almost dim now. The big handsome black girl that always sang in a red frock was no longer there. What a place Connor's was from 1914 to 1916 when that girl was singing and kicking and showing her bright green panties there! And the little ebony drummer, beloved of every cabaret lover in Harlem, was a fiend for rattling the drum!

Barron's was still Barron's, depending on its downtown white trade. Leroy's, the big common rendezvous shop for everybody. Edmond's still in the running. A fine new place that was opened in Brooklyn was freezing to death. Brooklyn never could support anything.

Goldgraben's on Lenox Avenue was leading

all the Negro cabarets a cruel dance. The big-spirited Jew had brought his cabaret up from the basement and established it in a hall blazing with lights, overlooking Lenox Avenue. He made a popular Harlem Negro manager. There the joy-loving ladies and gentlemen of the Belt collected to show their striking clothes and beautiful skin. Oh, it was some wonderful sight to watch them from the pavement! No wonder the lights of Connor's were dim. And Barron's had plunged deeper for the ofay trade. Goldgraben was grabbing all the golden-browns that had any spendable dough.

But the Congo remained in spite of formidable opposition and foreign exploitation. The Congo was a real throbbing little Africa in New York. It was an amusement place entirely for the unwashed of the Black Belt. Or, if they were washed, smells lingered telling the nature of their occupation. Pot-wrestlers, third cooks, W. C. attendants, scrub maids, dish-washers, stevedores.

Girls coming from the South to try their

future in New York always reached the Congo
first. The Congo was African in spirit and
color. No white persons were admitted there.
The proprietor knew his market. He did not
cater to the fast trade. "High yallers" were
scarce there. Except for such sweetmen that
lived off the low-down dark trade.

When you were fed up with the veneer of
Seventh Avenue, and Goldgraben's Afro-Ori-
ental garishness, you would go to the Congo
and turn rioting loose in all the tenacious
odors of service and the warm indigenous
smells of Harlem, fooping or jig-jagging the
night away. You would if you were a black
kid hunting for joy in New York.

Jake went down to the Baltimore. No sign
of his honey girl anywhere. He drank Scotch
after Scotch. His disappointment mounted
to anger against himself—turned to anger
against his honey girl. His eyes roved round
the room, but saw nobody.

"Oh what a big Ah-Ah I was!"

All round the den, luxuriating under the
little colored lights, the dark dandies were

loving up their pansies. Feet tickling feet under tables, tantalizing liquor-rich giggling,
hands busy above.

"Honey gal! Honey gal! What other sweet
boy is loving you now? Don't you know your
last night's daddy am waiting for you?"

The cabaret singer, a shiny coffee-colored
girl in a green frock and Indian-waved hair,
went singing from table to table in a man's
bass voice.

"You wanta know how I do it,
   How I look so good, how I am so happy,
All night on the blessed job—
   How I slide along making things go snappy?
      It is easy to tell,
      I ain't got no plan—
      But I'm crazy, plumb crazy
      About a man, mah man.

"It ain't no secret as you think,
   The glad heart is a state o' mind—
Throw a stone in the river and it will sink;
   But a feather goes whirling on the wind.
      It is easy to tell. . . ."

She stopped more than usual at Jake's table.
He gave her a half dollar. She danced a jag-

[31]

ging jig before him that made the giggles rise
like a wave in the room. The pansies stared
and tightened their grip on their dandies.
The dandies tightened their hold on themselves. They looked the favored Jake up and
down. All those perfection struts for him.
Yet he didn't seem aroused at all.

> "I'm crazy, plumb crazy
> About a man, mah man. . . ."

The girl went humming back to her seat.
She had poured every drop of her feeling into
the song.

> "Crazy, plumb crazy about a man, mah man. . . ."

Dandies and pansies, chocolate, chestnut,
coffee, ebony, cream, yellow, everybody was
teased up to the high point of excitement. . . .

> "Crazy, plumb crazy about a man, mah man. . . ."

The saxophone was moaning it. And feet
and hands and mouths were acting it. Dancing. Some jigged, some shuffled, some
walked, and some were glued together swaying on the dance floor.

Jake was going crazy. A hot fever was

burning him up. . . .Where was the singing gal that had danced to him? That dancing was for him all right. . . .

A crash cut through the music. A table went jazzing into the drum. The cabaret singer lay sprawling on the floor. A raging putty-skinned mulattress stamped on her ribs and spat in her face! "That'll teach you to leave mah man be every time." A black waiter rushed the mulattress. "Git off'n her. 'Causen she's down."

A potato-yellow man and a dull-black were locked. The proprietor, a heavy brown man, worked his elbow like a hatchet between them.

The antagonists glowered at each other.

"What you want to knock the gal down like that for, I acks you?"

"Better acks her why she done spits on mah woman."

"Woman! White man's wench, you mean. You low-down tripe. . . ."

The black man heaved toward the yellow, but the waiters hooked and hustled him off.

. . . Sitting at a table, the cabaret singer was soothing her eye.

"Git out on the sidewalk, all you trouble-makers," cried the proprietor. "And you, Bess," he cried to the cabaret singer, "nevah you show your face in mah place again."

The cabaret was closed for the rest of the night. Like dogs flicked apart by a whip-cord, the jazzers stood and talked resentfully in the street.

"Hi, Jake"—Zeddy, rocking into the group with a nosy air, spotted his buddy—"was you in on the li'l' fun?"

"Yes, buddy, but I wasn't mixed up in it. Sometimes they turn mah stomach, the womens. The same in France, the same in England, the same in Harlem. White against white and black against white and yellow against black and brown. We's all just crazy-dog mad. Ain't no peace on earth with the womens and there ain't no life anywhere without them."

"You said it, boh. It's a be-be itching life" —Zeddy scratched his flank—"and we're all

[34]

sons of it. . . . But what is you hitting round this joint? I thought you would be feeding off milk and honey tonight?"

"Hard luck, buddy. Done lose out counta mah own indiligence. I fohgit the street and the house. Thought I'd find her heah but. . . ."

"What you thinking 'bout, boh?"

"That gal got beat up in the Baltimore. She done sings me into a tantalizing mood. Ahm feeling like."

"Let's take a look in on the Congo, boh. It's the best pick-me-up place in Harlem."

"I'm with you, buddy."

"Always packed with the best pickings. When the chippies come up from down home, tha's where they hangs out first. You kain always find something that New York ain't done made a fool of yet. Theah's a high-yaller entertainer there that I'se got a crush on, but she ain't nevah gived me a encouraging eye."

[35]

"I ain't much for the high-yallers after having been so much fed-up on the ofays," said Jake. "They's so doggone much alike."

"Ah no, boh. A sweet-lovin' high-yaller queen's got something different. K-hhhhhhh, K-hhhhhhh. Something nigger."

The Congo was thick, dark-colorful, and fascinating. Drum and saxophone were fighting out the wonderful drag "blues" that was the favorite of all the low-down dance halls. In all the better places it was banned. Rumor said it was a police ban. It was an old tune, so far as popular tunes go. But at the Congo it lived fresh and green as grass. Everybody there was giggling and wriggling to it.

And it is ashes to ashes and dust to dust,
Can you show me a woman that a man can trust?

Oh, baby, how are you?
Oh, baby, what are you?
Oh, can I have you now,
Or have I got to wait?
Oh, let me have a date,
Why do you hesitate?

And there is two things in Harlem I don't understan'
It is a bulldycking woman and a faggotty man.

Oh, baby how are you?
Oh, baby, what are you? . . .

Jake and Zeddy picked two girls from a green bench and waded into the hot soup. The saxophone and drum fought over the punctuated notes. The cymbals clashed. The excitement mounted. Couples breasted each other in rhythmical abandon, grinned back at their friends and chanted:

"Oh, baby, how are you?
Oh, baby, what are you? . . ."

Clash! The cymbal snuffed out saxophone and drum, the dancers fell apart,—reeled, strutted, drifted back to their g r e e n places. . . .

Zeddy tossed down the third glass of Gordon gin and became aware of Rose, the Congo entertainer, singing at the table. Happy for the moment, he gave her fifty cents. She sang some more, but Zeddy saw that it was all for Jake. Finished, she sat down, uninvited, at their table.

How many nights, hungry nights, Zeddy

had wished that Rose would sit down voluntarily at his table. He had asked her sometimes. She would sit, take a drink and leave. Nothing doing. If he was a "big nigger," perhaps—but she was too high-priced for him. Now she was falling for Jake. Perhaps it was Jake's nifty suit. . . .

"Gin for mine," Rose said. Jake ordered two gins and a Scotch. "Scotch! That's an ofay drink," Rose remarked. "And I've seen the monkey-chasers order it when they want to put on style."

"It's good," Jake said. "Taste it."

She shook her head. "I have befoh. I don't like the taste. Gimme gin every time or good old red Kentucky."

"I got used to it over the other side," Jake said.

"Oh! You're an over-yonder baby! Sure enough!" She fondled his suit in admiration.

Zeddy, like a good understanding buddy, had slipped away. Another Scotch and Gordon Dry. The glasses kissed. Like a lean lazy leopard the mulattress reclined against Jake.

The milk cans were sounding on the pavements and a few pale stars were still visible in the sky when Rose left the Congo with both hands entwined in Jake's arm.

"You gwina stay with me, mah brown?"

"I ain't got me a room yet," he said.

"Come stay with me always. Got any stuff to bring along?"

"Mah suitcase at Uncle Doc's."

They went to her room in One Hundred and Thirty-third street. Locking the door, she said: "You remember the song they used to sing before you all went over there, mah brown?"

Softly she chanted:

"If I had some one like you at home
I wouldn't wanta go out, I wouldn't wanta go out. . . .
If I had some one like you at home,
I'd put a padlock on the door. . . ."

She hugged him to her.

"I love you. I ain't got no man."

[39]

"Gwan, tell that to the marines," he panted.

"Honest to God. Lemme kiss you nice."

It was now eating-time in Harlem. They were hungry. They washed and dressed.

"If you'll be mah man always, you won't have to work," she said.

"Me?" responded Jake. "I've never been a sweetman yet. Never lived off no womens and never will. I always works."

"I don't care what you do whilst you is mah man. But hard work's no good for a sweet-loving papa."

ON THE JOB AGAIN

V

*J*AKE stayed on in Rose's room. He could not feel about her as he did for his little lost maroon-brown of the Baltimore. He went frequently to the Baltimore, but he never saw her again. Then he grew to hate that cabaret and stopped going there.

The mulattress was charged with tireless activity and Jake was her big, good slave. But her spirit lacked the charm and verve, the infectious joy, of his little lost brown. He sometimes felt that she had no spirit at all— that strange, elusive something that he felt in himself, sometimes here, sometimes there, roaming away from him, going back to London, to Brest, Le Havre, wandering to some unknown new port, caught a moment by some romantic rhythm, color, face, passing through cabarets, saloons, speakeasies, and returning to him. . . . The little brown had something of

that in her, too. That night he had felt a
reaching out and marriage of spirits. . . . But
the mulattress was all a wonderful tissue of
throbbing flesh. He had never once felt in
her any tenderness or timidity or aloof-
ness. . . .

Jake was working longshore. Hooking barrels and boxes, wrestling with chains and
cranes. He didn't have a little-boss job this
time. But that didn't worry him. He
was one blackamoor that nourished a perfect
contempt for place. There were times when
he divided his days between Rose and Uncle
Doc's saloon and Dixie Red's pool-room.

He never took money from her. If he
gambled away his own and was short, he borrowed from Nije Gridley, the longshoreman
broker. Nije Gridley was a tall, thin, shiny
black man. His long eyelashes gave his sharp
eyes a sleepy appearance, but he was always
wide awake. Before Jake was shipped to
France, Nije had a rooming-house in Harlem's Fifth Avenue, worked a little at long-
shoring himself, and lent money on the checks

of the hard-gambling boys. Now he had three rooming-houses, one of which, free of mortgage, he owned. His lean belly bore a heavy gold chain and he strutted Fifth and Lenox in a ministerial crow-black suit. With the war boom of wages, the boys had gambled heavily and borrowed recklessly.

Ordinarily, Nije lent money at the rate of a dollar on four and two on eight per week. He complained bitterly of losses. Twenty-five dollars loaned on a check which, presented, brought only a day's pay. There were tough fellows that played him that game sometimes. They went and never returned to borrow again. But Nije's interest covered up such gaps. And sometimes he gave ten dollars on a forty-dollar check, drew the wages, and never saw his customer again, who had vanished entirely out of that phase of Harlem life.

One week when they were not working, Zeddy came to Jake with wonderful news. Men were wanted at a certain pier to unload pineapples at eight dollars a day. Eight dollars was exceptional wages, but the fruit was spoiling.

Jake went with Zeddy and worked the first day with a group of Negroes and a few white men. The white men were not regular dock workers. The only thing that seemed strange to Jake was that all the men ate inside and were not allowed outside the gates for lunch. But, on the second day, his primitive passion for going against regulation urged him to go out in the street after lunch.

Heaving casually along West Street, he was hailed by a white man. "Hello, fellow-worker!"

"Hello, there! What's up?" Jake asked.

"You working in there?"

"Sure I is. Since yestidday."

The man told Jake that there was a strike on and he was scabbing. Jake asked him why there were no pickets if there was a strike. The man replied that there were no pickets because the union leaders were against the strike, and had connived with the police to beat up and jail the pickets.

"Well, pardner," Jake said, "I've done worked through a tur'ble assortaments o' jobs in mah lifetime, but I ain't nevah yet scabbed it on any man. I done work in this heah country, and I works good and hard over there in France. I works in London and I nevah was a blackleg, although I been the only black man in mah gang."

"Fine, fellow-worker; that's a real man's talk," said the white man. He took a little red book out of his pocket and asked Jake to let him sign him up in his union.

"It's the only one in the country for a redblooded worker, no matter what race or nation he belongs to."

"Nope, I won't scab, but I ain't a joiner kind of a fellah," said Jake. "I ain't no white folks' nigger and I ain't no poah white's fool. When I longshored in Philly I was a good union man. But when I made New York I done finds out that they gived the colored mens the worser piers and holds the bes'n a' them foh the Irishmen. No, pardner, keep you' card. I take the best I k'n get as I goes

mah way. But I tells you, things ain't none at
all lovely between white and black in this heah
Gawd's own country."

"We take all men in our union regardless
——" But Jake was haunching along out of
hearing down West Street. . . . Suddenly he
heard sharp, deep, distressful grunts, and saw
behind some barrels a black man down and
being kicked perilously in the rear end by two
white men. Jake drew his hook from his belt
and, waving it in the air, he rushed them. The
white men shot like rats to cover. The down
man scrambled to his feet. One of Zeddy's
pals, Jake recognized him.

"What's the matter, buddy, the peckawoods
them was doing you in?"

"Becaz they said there was a strike in theah.
And I said I didn't give a doughnut, I was
going to work foh mah money all the same. I
got one o' them bif! in the eye, though. . . ."

"Don't go back, buddy. Let the boss-men
stick them jobs up. They are a bunch of rotten aigs. Just using us to do their dirty work.

[46]

Come on, let's haul bottom away from here to Harlem."

At Dixie Red's pool-room that evening there were some fellows with bandaged arms and heads. One iron-heavy, blue-black lad (he was called Liver-lip behind his back, because of the plankiness of his lips) carried his arm in a sling, and told Jake how he happened to be like that.

"They done jumped on me soon as I turned mah black moon on that li'l saloon tha's catering to us niggers. Heabenly God! But if the stars them didn't twinkle way down in mah eyes. But easy, easy, old man, I got out mah shaving steel and draws it down the goosey flesh o' one o' them, and, buddy, you shoulda heah him squeal. . . . The pohlice?" His massive mouth molded the words to its own form. "They tooks me, yes, but tunned me loose by'n'by. They's with us this time, boh, but, Lawdy! if they hadn't did entervention I woulda gutted gizzard and kidney outa that white tripe."

Jake was angry with Zeddy and asked him,

when he came in, why he had not told him at
first that the job was a scab job.

"I won't scab on nobody, not even the or-
neriest crackers," he said.

"Bull Durham!" cried Zeddy. "What was
I going to let on about anything for? The
boss-man done paid me to git him mens, and
I got them. Ain't I working there mahself?
I'll take any job in this heah Gawd's country
that the white boss make it worf mah while to
work at."

"But it ain't decent to scab," said Jake.

"Decent mah black moon!" shouted Zeddy.
"I'll scab through hell to make mah living.
Scab job or open shop or union am all the
same jobs to me. White mens don't want niggers in them unions, nohow. Ain't you a good
carpenter? And ain't I a good blacksmith?
But kain we get a look-in on our trade heah
in this white man's city? Ain't white mens
done scabbed niggers outa all the jobs they
useter hold down heah in this city? Waiter,
bootblack, and barber shop?"

"With all a that scabbing is a low-down deal," Jake maintained.

"Me eye! Seems lak youse gittin' religion, boh. Youse talking death, tha's what you sure is. One thing I know is niggers am made foh life. And I want to live, boh, and feel plenty o' the juice o' life in mah blood. I wanta live and I wanta love. And niggers am got to work hard foh that. Buddy, I'll tell you this and I'll tell it to the wo'l'—all the crackers, all them poah white trash, all the nigger-hitting and nigger-breaking white folks—I loves life and I got to live and I'll scab through hell to live."

Jake did not work again that week. By Saturday morning he didn't have a nickel, so he went to Nije Gridley to borrow money. Nije asked him if he was going that evening to Billy Biasse's railroad flat, the longshoremen gaming rendezvous. Jake said no, he was going with Zeddy to a buffet flat in One Hundred and Fortieth Street. The buffet flat was the rendezvous of a group of railroad porters and club waiters who gambled for big stakes. Jake did not go there often because he had to dress up as if he were going to a cabaret. Also, he was not a big-stake gambler. . . . He preferred Billy Biasse's, where he could go whenever he liked with hook and overalls.

"Oh, that's whar Zeddy's hanging out now," Nije commented, casually.

For some time before Jake's return from Europe Zeddy had stopped going to Billy Biasse's. He told Jake he was fed up with it. Jake did not know that Zeddy owed Nije money and that he did not go to Billy Biasse's because Nije often went there. . . .

Later in the evening Nije went to Billy Biasse's and found a longshoreman who was known at the buffet flat, to take him there.

Gambling was a bigger game than sex at this buffet flat. The copper-hued lady who owned it was herself a very good poker-player. There were only two cocoa-brown girls there. Not young or attractive. They made a show of doing something, serving drinks and trying hard to make jokes. In dining- and sitting-room, five tables were occupied by card-players. Railroad porters, long-shoremen, waiters; tight-faced, anxious-eyed. Zeddy sat at the same table with the lady of the flat. He had just eliminated two cards and asked for two when Nije and his escort were let into the flat. Zeddy smelled his man and knew it was Nije without looking up.

Nije swaggered past Zeddy and joined a group at another table. The gaming went on with intermittent calls for drinks. Nije sat where he could watch Zeddy's face. Zeddy also, although apparently intent on the cards, kept a wary eye on Nije. Sometimes their eyes met. No one was aware of the challenge that was developing between the two men.

There was a little slackening in the games, a general call for drinks, and a shifting of chairs. Nije got nearer to Zeddy. . . . Half-smiling and careless-like, he planted his boot-heel upon Zeddy's toes.

"Git off mah feets," Zeddy barked. The answer was a hard blow in the face. Zeddy tasted blood in his mouth. He threw his muscular gorilla body upon the tall Nije and hugged him down to the floor.

"You blasted black Jew, say you' prayers!" cried Zeddy.

"Ain't scared o' none o' you barefaced robber niggers." Nije was breathing hard under Zeddy and trying to get the better of him by the help of the wall.

"Black man," growled Zeddy, "I'se gwineta cut your throat just so sure as God is white."

With his knee upon Nije's chest and his left hand on his windpipe, Zeddy flashed the deadly-gleaming blade out of his back pocket. The proprietress let loose a blood-curdling scream, but before Zeddy's hand could achieve its purpose, Jake aimed a swift kick at his elbow. The razor flew spinning upward and fell chopping through a glass of gin on the pianola.

The proprietress fell upon Zeddy and clawed at him. "Wha's the matter all you bums trying to ruin mah place?" she cried. "Ain't I been a good spoht with you all, making everything here nice and respectable?"

Jake took charge of Zeddy. Two men hustled Nije off away out of the flat.

"Who was it put the krimp on me?" asked Zeddy.

"You ought to praise the Lawd you was saved from Sing Sing and don't ask no questions," the woman replied.

Everybody was talking.

"How did that long, tall, blood-suckin' nigger get in heah?"

"Soon as this heah kind a business stahts, the dicks will sartain sure git on to us."

"It ain't no moh than last week they done raided Madame Jerkin's, the niftiest buffet flat in Harlem. O Lawdy!"

"That ole black cock," growled Zeddy, "he wouldn'a' crowed round Harlem no moh after I'd done made that theah fine blade talk in his throat."

"Shut up you," the proprietress said, "or I'll throw you out." And Zeddy, the ape, who was scared of no man in the place, became humble before the woman. She began setting the room to order, helped by the two cocoa-

[53]

brown girls. A man shuffling a pack of cards called to Zeddy and Jake.

But the woman held up her hand. "No more card-playing tonight. I feel too nervous."

"Let's dance, then," suggested the smaller cocoa-brown girl.

A "blues" came trotting out of the pianola. The proprietress bounced into Jake's arms. The men sprang at the two girls. The unlucky ones paired off with each other.

Oh, "blues," "blues," "blues." Black-framed white grinning. Finger-snapping. Undertone singing. The three men with women teasing the stags. Zeddy's gorilla feet dancing down the dark death lurking in his heart. Zeddy dancing with a pal. "Blues," "blues," "blues." Red moods, black moods, golden moods. Curious, syncopated slipping-over into one mood, back-sliding back to the first mood. Humming in harmony, barbaric harmony, joy-drunk, chasing out the shadow of the moment before.

VI

ZEDDY was excited over Jake's success in love. He thought how often he had tried to make up to Rose, without succeeding. He was crazy about finding a woman to love him for himself.

He had been married when he was quite a lad to a crust-yellow girl in Petersburg. Zeddy's wife, after deceiving him with white men, had run away from him to live an easier life. That was before Zeddy came North. Since then he had had many other alliances. But none had been successful.

It was true that no Black Belt beauty would ever call Zeddy "mah han'some brown." But there were sweetmen of the Belt more repulsive than he, that women would fight and murder each other for. Zeddy did not seem to possess any of that magic that charms and holds women for a long time. All his at-

[55]

tempts at home-making had failed. The women left him when he could not furnish the cash to meet the bills. They never saw his wages. For it was gobbled up by his voracious passion for poker and crap games. Zeddy gambled in Harlem. He gambled with white men down by the piers. And he was always losing.

"If only I could get those kinda gals that falls foh Jake," Zeddy mused. "And Jake is such a fool spade. Don't know how to handle the womens."

Zeddy's chance came at last. One Saturday a yellow-skinned youth, whose days and nights were wholly spent between pool-rooms and Negro speakeasies, invited Zeddy to a sociable at a grass-widow's who lived in Brooklyn and worked as a cook downtown in New York. She was called Gin-head Susy. She had a little apartment in Myrtle Avenue near Prince Street.

Susy was wonderfully created. She was of the complexion known among Negroes as spade or chocolate-to-the-bone. Her eyes

shone like big white stars. Her chest was majestic and the general effect like a mountain.
And that mountain was overgrand because
Susy never wore any other but extremely
French-heeled shoes. Even over the range
she always stood poised in them and blazing
in bright-hued clothes.

The burning passion of Susy's life was the
yellow youth of her race. Susy came from
South Carolina. A yellow youngster married
her when she was fifteen and left her before
she was eighteen. Since then she had lived
with a yellow complex at the core of her heart.

Civilization had brought strikingly exotic
types into Susy's race. And like many, many
Negroes, she was a victim to that. . . . Ancient black life rooted upon its base with all
its fascinating new layers of brown, low-
brown, high-brown, nut-brown, lemon, maroon, olive, mauve, gold. Yellow balancing
between black and white. Black reaching out
beyond yellow. Almost-white on the brink of
a change. Sucked back down into the current

of black by the terribly sweet rhythm of black blood. . . .

Susy's life of yellow complexity was surcharged with gin. There were whisky and beer also at her sociable evenings, but gin was the drink of drinks. Except for herself, her parties were all-male. Like so many of her sex, she had a congenital contempt for women. All-male were her parties and as yellow as she could make them. A lemon-colored or paper-brown pool-room youngster from Harlem's Fifth Avenue or from Prince Street. A bell-boy or railroad waiter or porter. Sometimes a chocolate who was a quick, nondiscriminating lover and not remote of attitude like the pampered high-browns. But chocolates were always a rarity among Susy's front-roomful of gin-lovers.

Yet for all of her wages drowned in gin, Susy carried a hive of discontents in her majestic breast. She desired a lover, something like her undutiful husband, but she desired in vain. Her guests consumed her gin and listened to the phonograph, exchanged rakish stories, and when they felt fruit-ripe to dropping, left her place in pursuit of pleasures elsewhere.

Sometimes Susy managed to lay hold of a yellow one for some time. Something all a piece of dirty rags and stench picked up in the street. Cleansed, clothed, and booted it. But so soon as he got his curly hair straightened by the process of Harlem's Ambrozine Palace of Beauty, and started in strutting the pavement of Lenox Avenue, feeling smart as a moving-picture dandy, he would leave Susy.

Apart from Susy's repellent person, no youthful sweetman attempting to love her could hold out under the ridicule of his pals. Over their games of pool and craps the boys had their cracks at Susy.

"What about Gin-head Susy tonight?"

"Sure, let's go and look the crazy old broad over."

"I'll go anywheres foh swilling of good booze."

"She's sho one ugly spade, but she's right there with her Gordon Dry."

"She ain't got 'em from creeps to crown and her trotters is B flat, but her gin is regal."

But now, after all the years of gin sociables and unsatisfactory lemons, Susy was changing just a little. She was changing under the influence of her newly-acquired friend, Lavinia Curdy, the only woman whom she tolerated at her parties. That was not so difficult, as Miss Curdy was less attractive than Susy. Miss Curdy was a putty-skinned mulattress with purple streaks on her face. Two of her upper front teeth had been knocked out and her lower lip slanted pathetically leftward. She was skinny and when she laughed she resembled an old braying jenny.

When Susy came to know Miss Curdy, she unloaded a quantity of the stuff of her breast upon her. Her drab childhood in a South Carolina town. Her early marriage. No girlhood. Her husband leaving her. And all the yellow men that had beaten her, stolen from her, and pawned her things.

Miss Curdy had been very emphatic to Susy about "yaller men." "I know them from long experience. They never want to work. They're a lazy and shiftless lot. Want to be kept like women. I found that out a long, long time ago. And that's why when I wanted a man foh keeps I took me a black plug-ugly one, mah dear."

It wouldn't have supported the plausibility of Miss Curdy's advice if she had mentioned that more than one black plug-ugly had ruthlessly cut loose from her. As the black woman had had her entanglements in yellow, so had the mulattress hers of black. But, perhaps, Miss Curdy did not realize that she could not help desiring black. In her salad days as a business girl her purse was controlled by many a black man. Now, however, her old problems did not arise in exactly the same way,— her purse was old and worn and flat and attracted no attention.

"A black man is as good to me as a yaller when I finds a real one." Susy lied a little

[61]

to Miss Curdy from a feeling that she ought to show some pride in her own complexion.

"But all these sociables—and you spend so much coin on gin," Miss Curdy had said.

"Well, that's the trute, but we all of us drinks it. And I loves to have company in mah house, plenty of company."

But when Susy came home from work one evening and found that her latest "yaller" sweetie had stolen her suitcase and best dresses and pawned even her gas range, she resolved never to keep another of his kind as a "steady." At least she made that resolve to Miss Curdy. But the sociables went on and the same types came to drink the Saturday evenings away, leaving the two women at the finish to their empty bottles and glasses. Once Susy did make a show of a black lover. He was the house man at the boarding-house where she cooked. But the arrangement did not hold any time, for Susy demanded of the chocolate extremely more than she ever got from her yellows.

"Well, boh, we's Brooklyn bound tonight," said Zeddy to Jake.

"You got to show me that Brooklyn's got any life to it," replied Jake.

"Theah's life anywheres theah's booze and jazz, and theah's cases o' gin and a gramophone whar we's going."

"Has we got to pay foh it, buddy?"

"No, boh, eve'ything is f. o. c. ef the lady likes you."

"Blimey!" A cockney phrase stole Jake's tongue. "Don't bull me."

"I ain't. Honest-to-Gawd Gordon Dry, and moh—ef you're the goods, all f. o. c."

"Well, I'll be browned!" exclaimed Jake.

Zeddy also took along Strawberry Lips, a new pal, burnt-cork black, who was thus nicknamed from the peculiar stage-red color of his mouth. Strawberry Lips was typically the stage Negro. He was proof that a generalization has some foundation in truth. . . . You might live your life in many black belts and arrive at the conclusion that there is no such thing as a typical Negro—no minstrel coon off the stage, no Thomas Nelson Page's nigger, no Octavus Roy Cohen's porter, no lineal descendant of Uncle Tom. Then one day your theory may be upset through meeting with a type by far more perfect than any created counterpart.

"Myrtle Avenue used to be a be-be itching of a place," said Strawberry Lips, "when Doc Giles had his gambling house on there and Elijah Bowers was running his cabaret. H'm. But Bowers was some big guy. He knew swell white folks in politics, and had a grand automobile and a high-yaller wife that hadn't no need of painting to pass. His cabaret was running neck and neck with Marshall's in Fifty-third Street. Then one night he killed a man in his cabaret, and that finished him. The lawyers got him off. But they cleaned him out dry. Done broke him, that case did. And today he's plumb down and out."

Jake, Zeddy, and Strawberry Lips had left the subway train at Borough Hall and were walking down Myrtle Avenue.

"Bowers' cabaret was some place for the

teasing-brown pick-me-up then, brother—and the snow. The stuff was cheap then. You sniff, boh?" Strawberry Lips asked Jake and Zeddy.

"I wouldn't know befoh I sees it," Jake laughed.

"I ain't no habitual prisoner," said Zeddy, "but I does any little thing for a change. Keep going and active with anything, says I."

The phonograph was discharging its brassy jazz notes when they entered the apartment. Susy was jerking herself from one side to the other with a potato-skinned boy. Miss Curdy was half-hopping up and down with the only chocolate that was there. Five lads, ranging from brown to yellow in complexion, sat drinking with jaded sneering expressions on their faces. The one that had invited Zeddy was among them. He waved to him to come over with his friends.

"Sit down and try some gin," he said. . . .

Zeddy dipped his hand in his pocket and sent two bones rolling on the table.

"Ise with you, chappie," his yellow friend

said. The others crowded around. The gramophone stopped and Susy, hugging a bottle, came jerking on her French heels over to the group. She filled the glasses and everybody guzzled gin.

Miss Curdy looked the newcomers over, paying particular attention to Jake. A sure-enough eye-filling chocolate, she thought. I would like to make a steady thing of him.

Over by the door two light-brown lads began arguing about an actress of the leading theater of the Black Belt.

"I tell you I knows Gertie Kendall. I know her more'n I know you."

"Know her mah granny. You knows her just like I do, from the balcony of the Lafayette. Don't hand me none o' that fairy stuff, for I ain't gwine to swallow it."

"Youse an aching pain. I knows her, I tell you. I even danced with her at Madame Mulberry's apartment. You thinks I only hangs out with low-down trash becassin Ise in a place like this, eh? I done met mos'n all our big niggers: Jack Johnson, James Reese Europe, Adah Walker, Buddy, who used to play that theah drum for them Castle Walkers, and Madame Walker."

"Yaller, it 'pears to me that youse jest a na-cherally-born story-teller. You really spec's me to believe youse been associating with the mucty-mucks of the race? Gwan with you. You'll be telling me next you done speaks with Charlie Chaplin and John D. Rockefeller——"

Miss Curdy had tuned her ears to the conversation and broke in: "Why, what is that to make so much fuss about? Sure he can dance with Gertie Kendall and know the dickty niggers. In my sporting days I knew Bert Williams and Walker and Adah Overton and Editor Tukslack and all that upstage race gang that wouldn't touch Jack Johnson with a ten-foot pole. I lived in Washington and had Congressmen for my friends—foop! Why you can get in with the top-crust crowd at any swell ball in Harlem. All you need is clothes and the coin. I know them all, yet

I don't feel a bit haughty mixing here with Susy and you all."

"I guess you don't now," somebody said.

Gin went round . . . and round . . . and round. . . . Desultory dancing. . . . Dice. . . . Blackjack. . . . Poker. . . . The room became a close, live, intense place. Tight-faced, the men seemed interested only in drinking and gaming, while Susy and Miss Curdy, guzzling hard, grew uglier. A jungle atmosphere pervaded the room, and, like shameless wild animals hungry for raw meat, the females savagely searched the eyes of the males. Susy's eyes always came back to settle upon the lad that had invited Zeddy. He was her real object. And Miss Curdy was ginned up with high hopes of Jake.

Jake threw up the dice and Miss Curdy seized her chance to get him alone for a little while.

"The cards do get so tiresome," she said. "I wonder how you men can go on and on all night long poking around with poker."

"Better than worser things," retorted Jake. Disgusted by the purple streaks, he averted his eyes from the face of the mulattress.

"I don't know about that," Miss Curdy bridled. "There's many nice ways of spending a sociable evening between ladies and gentlemen."

"Got to show me," said Jake, simply because the popular phrase intrigued his tongue.

"And that I can."

Irritated, Jake turned to move away.

"Where you going? Scared of a lady?"

Jake recoiled from the challenge, and shuffled away from the hideous mulattress. From experience in seaport towns in America, in France, in England, he had concluded that a woman could always go farther than a man in coarseness, depravity, and sheer cupidity. Men were ugly and brutal. But beside women they were merely vicious children. Ignorant about the aim and meaning and fulfillment of life; uncertain and indeterminate; weak.

Rude children who loved excelling in spectacular acts to win the applause of women.

But women were so realistic and straight-going. *They* were the real controlling force of life. Jake remembered the bal-musette fights between colored and white soldiers in France. Blacks, browns, yellows, whites. . . . He remembered the interracial sex skirmishes in England. Men fought, hurt, wounded, killed each other. Women, like blazing torches, egged them on or denounced them. Victims of sex, the men seemed foolish, ape-like blunderers in their pools of blood. Didn't know what they were fighting for, except it was to gratify some vague feeling about women. . . .

Jake's thoughts went roaming after his little lost brown of the Baltimore. The difference! She, in one night, had revealed a fine different world to him. Mystery again. A little stray girl. Finer than the finest!

Some of the fellows were going. In a vexed spirit, Susy had turned away from her unresponsive mulatto toward Zeddy. Relieved, the mulatto yawned, threw his hands backwards and said: "I guess mah broad is home from Broadway by now. Got to final on home to her. Harlem, lemme see you."

Miss Curdy was sitting against the mantelpiece, charming Strawberry Lips. Marvellous lips. Salmon-pink and planky. She had hoisted herself upon his knees, her arm around his thick neck.

Jake went over to the mantelpiece to pour a large chaser of beer and Miss Curdy leered at him. She disgusted him. His life was a free coarse thing, but he detested nastiness and ugliness. Guess I'll haul bottom to Harlem, he thought. Congo Rose was a rearing wild animal, all right, but these women, these boys. . . . Skunks, tame skunks, all of them!

He was just going out when a chocolate lad pointed at a light-brown and said: "The pot calls foh four bits, chappie. Come across or stay out."

"Lemme a quarter!"

"Ain't got it. Staying out?"

Biff! Square on the mouth. The chocolate leaped up like a tiger-cat at his assailant,
carrying over card table, little pile of money,
and half-filled gin glasses with a crash. Like
an enraged ram goat, he held and butted the
light-brown boy twice, straight on the forehead. The victim crumpled with a thud to
the floor. Susy jerked over to the felled boy
and hauled him, his body leaving a liquid
trail, to the door. She flung him out in the
corridor and slammed the door.

"Sarves him right, pulling off that crap in
mah place. And you, Mis'er Jack Johnson," she said to the chocolate youth, "lemme
miss you quick."

"He done hits me first," the chocolate said.

"I knows it, but I ain't gwina stand foh no
rough-house in mah place. Ise got a dawg
heah wif me all ready foh bawking."

"K-hhhhh, K-hhhhh," laughed Strawberry
Lips. "Oh, boh, I know it's the trute,
but——"

The chocolate lad slunk out of the flat.

"Lavinia," said Susy to Miss Curdy, "put on that theah 'Tickling Blues' on the victroly."

The phonograph began its scraping and Miss Curdy started jig-jagging with Strawberry Lips. Jake gloomed with disgust against the door.

"Getting outa this, buddy?" he asked Zeddy.

"Nobody's chasing *us,* boh." Zeddy commenced stepping with Susy to the "Tickling Blues."

Outside, Jake found the light-brown boy still half-stunned against the wall.

"Ain't you gwine at home?" Jake asked him.

"I can't find a nickel foh car fare," said the boy.

Jake took him into a saloon and bought him a lemon squash. "Drink that to clear you' haid," he said. "And heah's car fare." He gave the boy a dollar. "Whar you living at?"

"San Juan Hill."

"Come on, le's git the subway, then."

The Myrtle Avenue Elevated train passed with a high raucous rumble over their heads.

"Myrtle Avenue," murmured Jake. "Pretty name, all right, but it stinks like a sewer. Legs and feets! Come take me outa it back home to Harlem."

VII

ZEDDY was scarce in Harlem. And Strawberry Lips was also scarce. It was fully a week after the Myrtle Avenue gin-fest before Jake saw Zeddy again. They met on the pavement in front of Uncle Doc's saloon.

"Why, where in the sweet name of niggers in Harlem, buddy, you been keeping you'-self?"

"Whar you think?"

"Think? I been very much thinking that Nije Gridley done git you."

"How come you git thataway, boh? Nije Gridley him ain't got a chawnst on the carve or the draw ag'inst Zeddy Plummer so long as Ise got me a black moon."

"Well, what's it done git you, then?"

"Myrtle Avenue."

"Come outa that; you ain't talking. . . ."

"The trute as I knows it, buddy."

[75]

"Crazy dog bite mah laig!" cried Jake. "You ain't telling me that you done gone. . . ."

"Transfer mah suitcase and all mah pohsitions to Susy."

"Gin-head Susy!"

"Egsactly; that crechur is mah ma-ma now. I done express mahself ovah theah on that very mahv'lously hang-ovah afternoon of that ginnity mawnin' that you left me theah. And Ise been right theah evah since."

"Well, Ise got to wish you good luck, buddy, although youse been keeping it so dark."

"It's the darkness of new loving, boh. But the honeymoon is good and well ovah, and I'll be li'l moh in Harlem as usual, looking the chippies and chappies ovah. I ain't none at all stuck on Brooklyn."

"It's a swah hole all right," said Jake.

"But theah's sweet stuff in it." Zeddy tongue-wiped his fleshy lips with a salacious laugh.

"It's all right, believe me, boh," he informed Jake. "Susy ain't nothing to look at like you' fair-brown queen, but she's tur'bly sweet loving. You know when a ma-ma ain't the goods in looks and figure, she's got to make up foh it some. And that Susy does. And she treats me right. Gimme all I wants to drink and brings home the goodest poke chops and fried chicken foh me to put away under mah shirt. . . . Youse got to come and feed with us all one o' these heah evenings."

It was a party of five when Jake went again to Myrtle Avenue for the magnificent free-love feast that Susy had prepared. It was Susy's free Sunday. Miss Curdy and Strawberry Lips were also celebrating. Susy had concocted a pitcherful of knock-out gin cocktails. And such food! Susy could cook. Perhaps it was her splendid style that made her sink all her wages in gin and sweetmen. For she belonged to the ancient aristocracy of black cooks, and knew that she was always sure of a good place, so long as the palates of rich Southerners retained their discriminating taste.

Cream tomato soup. Ragout of chicken giblets. Southern fried chicken. Candied sweet potatoes. Stewed corn. Rum-flavored fruit salad waiting in the ice-box. . . . The stars rolling in Susy's shining face showed how pleased she was with her art.

She may be fat and ugly as a turkey, thought Jake, but her eats am sure beautiful.

"Heah! Pass me you' plate," Susy gave Jake a leg. Zeddy held out his plate again and got a wing. Strawberry Lips received a bit of breast. . . .

"No more chicken for me, Susy," Miss Curdy mumbled, "but I *will* have another helping of that there stewed corn. I don't know what ingredients yo-all puts in it, but, Lawdy! I never tasted anything near so good."

Susy beamed and dipped up three spoon-fuls of corn. "Plenty, thank you," Miss Curdy stopped her from filling up her saucer. . . . Susy drank off a tumbler of cocktail at a draught, and wiped her lips with the white serviette that was stuck into the low neck of her vermillion crepe-de-chine blouse. . . .

When Jake was ready to leave, Zeddy announced that he would take a little jaunt with him to Harlem.

"You ain'ta gwine to do no sich thing as that," Susy said.

"Yes I is," responded Zeddy. "Wha' there is to stop me?"

"I is," said Susy.

"And what foh?"

" 'Causen I don't wanchu to go to Harlem. What makes you niggers love Harlem so much? Because it's a bloody ungodly place where niggers nevah go to bed. All night running around speakeasies and cabarets, where bad, hell-bent nigger womens am giving up themselves to open sin."

Susy stood broad and aggressive against the window overlooking Myrtle Avenue.

"Harlem is all right," said Zeddy. "I ain't knocking round no cabarets and speakeasies. Ahm just gwine ovah wif Jake to see soma-them boys."

"Can that boy business!" cried Susy. "I've had anuff hell scrapping wif the women ovah mah mens. I ain't agwine to have no Harlem boys seducin' mah man away fwom me. The boy business is a fine excuse indeedy foh sich womens as ain't wise. I always heah the boss say to the missus, 'I gwine out foh a little time wif the boys, dearie.' when him wants an excuse foh a night off. I ain't born yestiday, honey. If you wants the boys foh a li'l' game o' poky, you bring 'em ovah heah. I ain't got the teeeniest bit of objection, and Ise got plenty o' good Gordon Dry foh eve'body."

"Ise got to go scares them up to bring them heah," said Zeddy.

"But not tonight or no night," declared Susy. "You kain do that in the daytime, foh you ain't got nothing to do."

Zeddy moved toward the mantelpiece to get his cap, but Susy blocked his way and held the cap behind her.

Zeddy looked savagely in her eyes and growled: "Come outa that, sistah, and gimme mah cap. It ain't no use stahting trouble."

Susy looked steadily in his eyes and chucked

the cap at him. "Theah's you cap, but ef you stahts leaving me nights you . . ."

"What will you do?" asked Zeddy.

"I'll put you' block in the street."

Zeddy's countenance fell flat from its high aggressiveness.

"Well s'long, eve'body," said Jake.

Zeddy put on his cap and rocked out of the apartment after him. In the street he asked Jake, "Think I ought to take a crack at Harlem with you tonight, boh?"

"Not ef you loves you' new home, buddy," Jake replied.

"Bull! That plug-ugly black woman is ornery like hell. I ain't gwineta let her bridle and ride me. . . . You ain't in no pickle like that with Rose, is you?"

"Lawd, no! I do as I wanta. But I'm one independent cuss, buddy. We ain't sitchuate the same. I works."

"Black womens when theyse ugly am all sistahs of Satan," declared Zeddy.

"It ain't the black ones only," said Jake.

"I wish I could hit things off like you,

boh," said Zeddy. . . . "Well, I'll see you all some night at Billy Biasse's joint. . . . S'long. Don't pick up no bad change."

From that evening Zeddy began to discover that it wasn't all fine and lovely to live sweet. Formerly he had always been envious when any of his pals pointed out an extravagantly-dressed dark dandy and remarked, "He was living sweet." There was something so romantic about the sweet life. To be the adored of a Negro lady of means, or of a pseudo grass-widow whose husband worked on the railroad, or of a hard-working laundress or cook. It was much more respectable and enviable to be sweet—to belong to the exotic aristocracy of sweetmen than to be just a common tout.

But there were strings to Susy's largesse. The enjoyment of Harlem's low night life was prohibited to Zeddy. Susy was jealous of him in the proprietary sense. She believed in free love all right, but not for the man she possessed and supported. She warned him against the ornery hussies of her race.

[82]

"Nigger hussies nevah wanta git next to a man 'cep'n' when he's a-looking good to another woman," Susy declared. "I done gived you fair warning to jest keep away from the buffet-flat widdahs and thim Harlem street floaters; foh ef I ketch you making a fool woman of me, I'll throw you' pants in the street."

"Hi, but youse talking sistah. Why don't you wait till you see something before you staht in chewing the rag?"

"I done give you the straight stuff in time so you kain watch you'self when I kain't watch you. I ain't bohding and lodging no black man foh'm to be any other nigger woman's daddy."

So, in a few pointed phrases, Susy let Zeddy understand precisely what she would stand for. Zeddy was well kept like a prince of his type. He could not complain about food . . . and bed. Susy was splendid in her matriarchal way, rolling her eyes with love or disapproval at him, according to the exigencies of the moment.

The Saturday-night gin parties went on as usual. The brown and high-brown boys came and swilled. Miss Curdy was a constant visitor, frequently toting Strawberry Lips along. About her general way of handling things Susy brooked no criticism from Zeddy. She had bargained with him in the interest of necessity and of rivalry and she paid and paid fully, but grimly. She was proud to have a man to boss about in an intimate, casual way.

"Git out another bottle of gin, Zeddy. . . ."

"Bring along that packet o' saltines. . . ."

"Put on that theah 'Tickling Blues' that we's all just crazy about."

To have an aggressive type like Zeddy at her beck and call considerably increased Susy's prestige and clucking pride. She noticed, with carefully-concealed delight, that the interest of the yellow gin-swillers was piqued. She became flirtatious and coy by turns. And she was rewarded by fresh attentions. Even Miss Curdy was now meeting with new adventures, and she was prompted to expatiate upon men and love to Susy.

"Men's got a whole lot of women in their nature, I tell you. Just as women never really see a man until he's looking good to another woman and the hussies want to steal him, it's the same thing with men, mah dear. So soon as a woman is all sugar and candy for another man, you find a lot of them heartbreakers all trying to get next to her. Like a set of strutting game cocks all priming themselves to crow over a li'l' piece o' nothing."

"That's the gospel trute indeed," agreed Susy. "I done have a mess of knowledge 'bout men tucked away heah." Susy tapped her head of tight-rolled kinks knotted with scraps of ribbon of different colors. "I pays foh what I know and I've nevah been sorry, either. Yes, mam, I done larned about mah own self fust. Had no allusions about mahself. I knowed that I was black and ugly and noclass and unejucated. And I knowed that I was bohn foh love. . . . Mah mammy did useter warn me about love. All what the white folks call white slavery theseadays. I dunno ef theah's another name foh the nigger-

[85]

an'-white side ovit down home in Dixie. Well,
I soon found out it wasn't womens alone in
the business, sposing thimselves like vigitables
foh sale in the market. No, mam! I done
soon l'arned that the mens was most buyable
thimselves. Mah heart-breaking high-yaller
done left me sence—how miny wintahs I been
counting this heah Nothan snow? All thim
and some moh—dawggone ef I remimber.
But evah since I been paying sistah, paying
good and hard foh mah loving feelings."

"Life ain't no country picnic with sweet
flute and fiddle," Miss Curdy sighed.

"Indeed not," Susy was emphatic. "It ain't
got nothing to do with the rubbish we l'arn at
Sunday school and the sweet snooziness I used
to lap up in thim blue-cover story books. My
God! the things I've seen! Working with
white folks, so dickty and high-and-mighty,
you think theyse nevah oncet naked and thim
feets nevah touch ground. Yet all the silks
and furs and shining diamonds can't hide the
misery a them lives. . . . Servants and heartbreakers from outside stealing the husband's

stuff. And all the men them that can't find no sweet-loving life at home. Lavinia, I done seen life."

"Me, too, I have seen the real life, mixing as I used to in *real* society," said Miss Curdy.

"I know society, too, honey, even though I only knows it watching from the servant window. And I know it ain't no different from *us*. It's the same life even ef they drink champagne and we drink gin."

"You said it and said it right," responded Miss Curdy.

Zeddy discovered that in his own circles in Harlem he had become something of a joke. It was known that he was living sweet. But his buddies talked about his lady riding him with a cruel bit.

"He was kept, all right," they said, "kept under 'Gin-head' Susy's skirt."

He had had to fight a fellow in Dixie Red's pool-room, for calling him a "skirt-man."

He was even teased by Billy Biasse or Billy, the Wolf, as he was nicknamed. Billy boasted

frankly that he had no time for women. Black
women, or the whole diversified world of the
sex were all the same to him.

"So Harlem, after the sun done set, has no
fun at all foh you, eh, boh?" Billy asked
Zeddy.

Zeddy growled something indistinct.

"Sweet with the bit in you' mouf. Black
woman riding her nigger. Great life, boh, ef
you don't weaken."

"Bull! Wha's the matter with you niggers,
anyhow?" Zeddy said in a sort of general
way. "Ain't it better than being a wolf?"

"Ise a wolf, all right, but I ain't a lone one,"
Billy grinned. "I guess Ise the happiest, well-
feddest wolf in Harlem. Oh, boy!"

Zeddy spent that evening in Harlem drinking with Jake and two more longshoremen at
Uncle Doc's saloon. Late in the night they
went to the Congo. Zeddy returned to Myrtle
Avenue, an hour before it was time for Susy
to rise, fully ginned up.

To Susy's "Whar you been?" he answered,
"Shut up or I'll choke you," staggered,

swayed, and swept from the dresser a vase of chrysanthemums that broke on the floor.

"Goddam fool flowers," he growled. "Why in hell didn't you put them out of the way, hey, you Suze?"

"Oh, keep quiet and come along to bed," said Susy.

A week later he repeated the performance, coming home with alarming symptoms of gin hiccough. Susy said nothing. After that Zeddy began to prance, as much as a short, heavy-made human could, with the bit out of his mouth. . . .

One Saturday night Susy's gin party was a sad failure. Nobody came beside Miss Curdy with Strawberry Lips. (Zeddy had left for Harlem in the afternoon.) They drank to themselves and played coon-can. Near midnight, when Miss Curdy was going, she said offhandedly, "I wouldn't mind sampling one of those Harlem cabarets now." Susy at once seized upon the idea.

"Sure. Let's go to Harlem for a change."

They caught the subway train for Harlem. Arrived there they gravitated to the Congo.

Before Susy left Myrtle Avenue, Zeddy was already at the Congo with a sweet, timid, satin-faced brown just from down home, that he had found at Aunt Hattie's and induced to go with him to the cabaret. Jake sat at Zeddy's table. Zeddy was determined to go the limit of independence, to show the boys that he was a cocky sweetman and no skirt-man. Plenty of money. He was treating. He wore an elegant nigger-brown sports suit and patent-leather shoes with cream-light spats such as all the sweet swells love to strut in. If Zeddy had only been taller, trimmer, and well-arched he would have been one of Harlem's dandiest sports.

His new-found brown had a glass of Virginia Dare before her; he was drinking gin. Jake, Scotch-and-soda; and Rose, who sat with them when she was not entertaining, had ordered White Rock. The night before, or rather the early morning after her job was done, she had gone on a champagne party and now she was sobering up.

Billy Biasse was there at a neighboring table with a longshoreman and a straw-colored boy who was a striking advertisement of the Ambrozine Palace of Beauty. The boy was made up with high-brown powder, his eyebrows were elongated and blackened up, his lips streaked with the dark rouge so popular in Harlem, and his carefully-straightened hair lay plastered and glossy under Madame Walker's absinthe-colored salve "for milady of fashion and color."

"Who's the doll baby at the Wolf's table?" Zeddy asked.

"Tha's mah dancing pardner," Rose answered.

"Another entertainer? The Congo is gwine along fast enough."

"You bet you," said Jake. "And the ofays will soon be nosing it out. Then we'll have to take a back seat."

"Who's the Wolf?" Timidly Zeddy's girl asked.

Zeddy pointed out Billy.

"But why Wolf?"

"Khhhhhhh — Khhhhhhhh . . ." Zeddy laughed. " 'Causen he eats his own kind."

It was time for Rose to dance. Her partner had preceded her to the open space and was standing, arm akimbo against the piano, talking to the pianist. The pianist was a slight-built, long-headed fellow. His face shone like anthracite, his eyes were arresting, intense, deep-yellow slits. He seemed in a continual state of swaying excitement, whether or not he was playing.

They were ready, Rose and the dancer-boy. The pianist began, his eyes toward the ceiling in a sort of savage ecstatic dream. Fiddler, saxophonist, drummer, and cymbalist seemed to catch their inspiration from him. . . .

When Luty dances, everything
  Is dancing in the cabaret.
The second fiddle asks the first:
  What makes you sound that funny way?
The drum talks in so sweet a voice,
  The cymbal answers in surprise,

The lights put on a brighter glow
    To match the shine of Luty's eyes.

For he's a foot-manipulating fool
    When he hears that crazy moan
    Come rolling, rolling outa that saxophone. . . .
Watch that strut; there's no keeping him cool
    When he's a-rearing with that saxophone. . . .
    Oh, the tearing, tantalizing tone!
    Of that moaning saxophone. . . .
      That saxophone. . . .
      That saxophone. . . .

They danced, Rose and the boy. Oh, they danced! An exercise of rhythmical exactness for two. There was no motion she made that he did not imitate. They reared and pranced together, smacking palm against palm, working knee between knee, grinning with real joy. They shimmied, breast to breast, bent themselves far back and shimmied again. Lifting high her short skirt and showing her green bloomers, Rose kicked. And in his tight nigger-brown suit, the boy kicked even with her. They were right there together, neither going beyond the other. . . .

And the pianist! At intervals his yellow

eyes, almost bloodshot, swept the cabaret with
a triumphant glow, gave the dancers a caressing look, and returned to the ceiling. Lean,
smart fingers beating barbaric beauty out of a
white frame. Brown bodies, caught up in the
wild rhythm, wiggling and swaying in their
seats.

> For he's a foot-manipulating fool
> When he hears that crazy moan
> Come rolling, rolling outa that saxophone. . . .
> > That saxophone. . . .
> > That saxophone. . . .

Rose was sipping her White Rock. Her
partner, at Billy's table, sucked his iced creme-
de-menthe through a straw. The high wave
of joyful excitement had subsided and the customers sat casually drinking and gossiping as
if they had not been soaring a minute before
in a realm of pure joy.

From his place, giving a good view of the
staircase, Zeddy saw two apparently familiar
long legs swinging down the steps. Sure
enough, he knew those big, thick-soled red
boots.

"Them feets look jest laka Strawberry Lips' own," he said to Jake. Jake looked and saw first Strawberry Lips enter the cabaret, with Susy behind balancing upon her French heels, and Miss Curdy. Susy was gorgeous in a fur coat of rich shiny black, like her complexion. Opened, it showed a cérise blouse and a yellow-and-mauve check skirt. Her head of thoroughly-straightened hair flaunted a green hat with a decoration of red ostrich plumes.

"Great balls of fire! Here's you doom, buddy," said Jake.

"Doom, mah granny," retorted Zeddy. "Ef that theah black ole cow come fooling near me tonight, I'll show her who's wearing the pants."

Susy did not see Zeddy until her party was seated. It was Miss Curdy who saw him first. She dug into Susy's side with her elbow and cried:

"For the love of Gawd, looka there!"

Susy's star eyes followed Miss Curdy's. She glared at Zeddy and fixed her eyes on the girl

[95]

with him for a moment. Then she looked away and grunted: "He thinks he's acting smart, eh? Him and I will wrastle that out to a salution, but I ain't agwine to raise no stink in heah."

"He's got some more nerve pulling off that low-down stuff, and on your money, too," said Miss Curdy.

"Who that?" asked Strawberry Lips.

"Ain't you seen your best friends over there?" retorted Miss Curdy.

Strawberry Lips waved at Zeddy and Jake, but they were deliberately keeping their eyes away from Susy's table. He got up to go to them.

"Where you going?" Miss Curdy asked.

"To chin wif ——"

A yell startled the cabaret. A girl had slapped another's face and replied to her victim's cry of pain with, "If you no like it you can lump it!"

"You low an' dutty bobbin-bitch!"

"Bitch is bobbin in you' sistah's coffin."

They were West Indian girls.

"I'll mek mah breddah beat you' bottom foh you."

"Gash it and stop you' jawing."

They were interrupted by another West Indian girl, who wore a pink-flowered muslin frock and a wide jippi-jappa hat from which charmingly hung two long ends of broad pea-green ribbon.

"It's a shame. Can't you act like decent English people?" she said. Gently she began pushing away the assaulted girl, who burst into tears.

"She come boxing me up ovah a dutty-black 'Merican coon."

"Mek a quick move or I'll box you bumbole ovah de moon," her assailant cried after her. . . .

"The monkey-chasers am scrapping," Zeddy commented.

"In a language all their own," said Jake.

"They are wild womens, buddy, and it's a wild language they're using, too," remarked a young West Indian behind Jake.

"Hmm! but theyse got the excitement

[97]

fever," a lemon-colored girl at a near table made her contribution and rocked and twisted herself coquettishly at Jake. . . .

Susy had already reached the pavement with Miss Curdy and Strawberry Lips. Susy breathed heavily.

"Lesh git furthest away from this low-down vice hole," she said. "Leave that plug-ugly nigger theah. I ain't got no more use foh him nohow."

"I never did have any time for Harlem," said Miss Curdy. "When I was high up in society all respectable colored people lived in Washington. There was no Harlem full a niggers then. I declare ——"

"I should think the nigger heaven of a theater downtown is better than anything in this heah Harlem," said Susy. "When we feels like going out, it's better we enjoy ourse'f in the li'l' corner the white folks 'low us, and then shuffle along back home. It's good and quiet ovah in Brooklyn."

"And we can have all the inside fun we need," said Miss Curdy.

[98]

"Brooklyn ain't no better than Harlem," said Strawberry Lips, running the words rolling off his tongue. "Theah's as much shooting-up and cut-up in Prince Street and ——"

"There ain't no compahrison atall," stoutly maintained Susy. "This here Harlem is a stinking sink of iniquity. Nigger hell! That's what it is. Looka that theah ugly black nigger loving up a scrimpy brown gal right befoh mah eyes. Jest daring me to turn raw and loose lak them monkey-chasing womens thisanight. But that I wouldn't do. I ain't a woman abandoned to sich publicity stunts. Not even though mah craw was full to bursting. Lemme see'm tonight. . . . Yessam, this heah Harlem is sure nigger hell. Take me way away from it."

When Zeddy at last said good night to his new-found brown, he went straight to an all-night barrel-house and bought a half a pint of whisky. He guzzled the liquor and smashed the flask on the pavement. Drew up his pants, tightened his belt and growled, "Now I'm ready for Susy."

He caught the subway train for Brooklyn. Only local trains were running and it was quite an hour and a half before he got home. He staggered down Myrtle Avenue well primed with the powerful stimulation of gin-and-whisky.

At the door of Susy's apartment he was met by his suitcase. He recoiled as from a blow struck at his face. Immediately he became sober. His eyes caught a little white tag attached to the handle. Examining it by the faint gaslight he read, in Susy's handwriting: "Kip owt that meen you."

Susy had put all Zeddy's belongings into the suitcase, keeping back what she had given him: two fancy-colored silk shirts, silk handkerchiefs, a mauve dressing-gown, and a box of silk socks.

"What he's got on that black back of his'n he can have," she had said while throwing the things in the bag.

Zeddy beat on the door with his fists.

"Wha moh you want?" Susy's voice bawled from within. "Ain'tchu got all you stuff theah? Gwan back where youse coming from."

"Lemme in and quit you joking," cried Zeddy.

"You ugly flat-footed zigaboo," shouted Susy, "may I ketch the 'lectric chair without conversion ef I 'low you dirty black pusson in mah place again. And you better git quick foh I staht mah dawg bawking at you."

Zeddy picked up his suitcase. "Come on, Mistah Bag. Le's tail along back to Harlem. Leave black woman 'lone wif her gin and ugly mug. Black woman is hard luck."

VIII

*T*HE blazing lights of the Baltimore were put out and the entrance was padlocked. Fifth Avenue and Lenox talked about nothing else. Buddy meeting buddy and chippie greeting chippie, asked: "Did you hear the news?" . . . "Well, what do you know about that?"

Yet nothing sensational had happened in the Baltimore. The police had not, on a certain night, swept into it and closed it up because of indecent doings. No. It was an indirect raid. Oh, and that made the gossip toothier! For the Baltimore was not just an ordinary cabaret. It had mortgages and policies in the best of the speakeasy places of the Belt. And the mass of Harlem held the Baltimore in high respect because (it was rumored and believed) it was protected by Tammany Hall.

Jake, since he had given up hoping about his lost brown, had stopped haunting the Baltimore, yet he had happened to be very much in on the affair that cost the Baltimore its license. Jake's living with Rose had, in spite of himself, projected him into a more elegant atmosphere of worldliness. Through Rose and her associates he had gained access to buffet flats and private rendezvous apartments that were called "nifty."

And Jake was a high favorite wherever he went. There was something so naturally beautiful about his presence that everybody liked and desired him. Buddies, on the slightest provocation, were ready to fight for him, and the girls liked to make an argument around him.

Jake had gained admission to Madame Adeline Suarez's buffet flat, which was indeed a great feat. He was the first longshoreman, colored or white, to tread that magnificent red carpet. Madame Suarez catered to sporty colored persons of consequence only and certain groups of downtown whites that used to

frequent Harlem in the good old pre-prohibi-
tion days.

"Ain't got no time for cheap- no-'count niggers," Madame Suarez often said. "Gimme
their room to their company any time, even if
they've got money to spend." Madame Suarez
came from Florida and she claimed Cuban
descent through her father. By her claim to
that exotic blood she moved like a queen
among the blue-veins of the colored sporting
world.

But Jake's rough charm could conquer anything.

"Ofay's mixing in!" he exclaimed to himself the first night he penetrated into Madame
Suarez's. "But ofay or ofay not, this here is
the real stuff," he reflected. And so many
nights he absented himself from the Congo
(he had no interest in Rose's art of flirting
money out of hypnotized newcomers) to lux-
uriate with charmingly painted pansies among
the colored cushions and under the soft, shaded
lights of Madame Suarez's speakeasy. It was
a new world for Jake and he took it easily.

That was his natural way, wherever he went, whatever new people he met. It had helped him over many a bad crossing at Brest at Havre and in London. . . . Take it easy . . . take life easy. Sometimes he was disgusted with life, but he was never frightened of it.

Jake had never seen colored women so carefully elegant as these rich-browns and yellow-creams at Madame Suarez's. They were fascinating in soft bright draperies and pretty pumps and they drank liquor with a fetching graceful abandon. Gin and whisky seemed to lose their barbaric punch in that atmosphere and take on a romantic color. The women's coiffure was arranged in different striking styles and their arms and necks and breasts tinted to emphasize the peculiar richness of each skin. One girl, who was the favorite of Madame Suarez, and the darkest in the group, looked like a breathing statue of burnished bronze. With their arresting poses and gestures, their deep shining painted eyes, they resembled the wonderfully beautiful pictures of women of ancient Egypt.

Here Jake brushed against big men of the
colored sporting world and their white
friends. That strange un-American world
where colored meets and mingles freely and
naturally with white in amusement basements,
buffet flats, poker establishments. Sometimes
there were two or three white women, who
attracted attention because they were white
and strange to Harlem, but they appeared like
faded carnations among those burning orchids
of a tropical race.

One night Jake noticed three young white
men, clean-shaven, flashily-dressed, who paid
for champagne for everybody in the flat. They
were introduced by a perfectly groomed dark-
brown man, a close friend of the boss of the
Baltimore. Money seemed worthless to them
except as a means of getting fun out of it.
Madame Suarez made special efforts to please
them. Showed them all of the buffet flat, even
her own bedroom. One of them, very freck-
led and red-haired, sat down to the piano and
jazzed out popular songs. The trio radiated

friendliness all around them. Danced with the colored beauties and made lively conversation with the men. They were gay and recklessly spendthrift. . . .

They returned on a Saturday night, between midnight and morning, when the atmosphere of Madame Suarez's was fairly bacchic and jazz music was snake-wriggling in and out and around everything and forcing everybody into amatory states and attitudes. The three young white men had two others with them. At the piano a girl curiously made up in mauve was rendering the greatest ragtime song of the day. Broadway was wild about it and Harlem was crazy. All America jazzed to it, and it was already world-famous. Already being jazzed perhaps in Paris and Cairo, Shanghai, Honolulu, and Java. It was a song about cocktails and cherries. Like this in some ways:

Take a juicy cocktail cherry,
  Take a dainty little bite,
And we'll all be very merry
  On a cherry drunk tonight.

We'll all be merry when you have a cherry,
  And we'll twine and twine like a fruitful vine,
Grape vine, red wine, babe mine, bite a berry,
    You taste a cherry and twine, rose vine, sweet wine.
      Cherry-ee-ee-ee-ee, cherry-ee-ee-ee-ee-ee, ee-ee-ee
      Cherry-ee-ee-ee-ee, cherry-ee-ee-ee-ee-ee, ee-ee-ee
      Grape vine, rose vine, sweet wine. . . .

Love is like a cocktail cherry,
  Just a fruity little bit,
And you've never yet been merry,
  If you've not been drunk on it.

We'll all be merry when you have. . . .

The women, carried away by the sheer rhythm of delight, had risen above their commercial instincts (a common trait of Negroes in emotional states) and abandoned themselves to pure voluptuous jazzing. They were gorgeous animals swaying there through the dance, punctuating it with marks of warm physical excitement. The atmosphere was charged with intensity and over-charged with currents of personal reaction. . . .

Then the five young white men unmasked as the Vice Squad and killed the thing.

Dicks! They had wooed and lured and solicited for their trade. For two weeks they had spilled money like water at the Baltimore. Sometimes they were accompanied by white girls who swilled enormous quantities of champagne and outshrieked the little ginned-up Negresses and mulattresses of the cabaret. They had posed as good fellows, regular guys, looking for a good time only in the Black Belt. They were wearied of the pleasures of the big white world, wanted something new —the primitive joy of Harlem.

So at last, with their spendthrift and charming ways, they had convinced the wary boss of the Baltimore that they were fine fellows. The boss was a fine fellow himself, who loved life and various forms of fun and had no morals about them. And so one night when the trio had left their hired white ladies behind, he was persuaded to give his youthful white guests an introduction to Madame Adeline Suarez's buffet flat. . . .

The uniformed police were summoned.

Madame Suarez and her clients were ordered to get ready to go down to the Night Court. The women asked permission to veil themselves. Many windows were raked up in the block and heads craned forth to watch the prisoners bundled into waiting taxicabs. The women were afraid. Some of them were false grass-widows whose husbands were working somewhere. Some of them were church members. Perhaps one could claim a place in local society!

They were all fined. But Madame Suarez, besides being fined, was sent to Blackwell's Island for six months.

To the two white girls that were also taken in the raid the judge remarked that it was a pity he had no power to order them whipped. For whipping was the only punishment he considered suitable for white women who dishonored their race by associating with colored persons.

The high point of the case was the indictment of the boss of the Baltimore as accessory to the speakeasy crime. The boss was not convicted, but the Baltimore was ordered to be padlocked. That decision was appealed. But the cabaret remained padlocked. A black member of Tammany had no chances against the Moral Arm of the city.

The Belt's cabaret sets licked their lips over the sensation for weeks. For a long time Negro proprietors would not admit white customers into their cabarets and near-white members of the black race, whose features were unfamiliar in Harlem, had a difficult time proving their identity.

IX

COMING home from work one afternoon, Jake remarked a taxicab just driving away from his house. He was quite a block off, but he thought it was his number. When he entered Rose's room he immediately detected an unfamiliar smell. He had an uncanny sharp nose for strange smells. Rose always had visitors, of course. Girls, and fellows, too, of her circle. But Jake had a feeling that his nose had scented something foreign to Harlem. The room was close with tobacco smoke; there were many Melachrino butts in a tray, and a half-used box of the same cigarettes on a little table drawn up against the scarlet-covered couch. Also, there was a half-filled bottle of Jake's Scotch whisky on the table and glasses for two. Rose was standing before the dresser, arranging her hair.

"Been having company?" Jake asked, carelessly.

"Yep. It was only Gertie Blake."

Jake knew that Rose was lying. Her visitor had not been Gertie Blake. It had been a man, a strange man, doubtless a white man. Yet he hadn't the slightest feeling of jealousy or anger, whatever the visitor was. Rose had her friends of both sexes and was quite free in her ways. At the Congo she sat and drank and flirted with many fellows. That was a part of her business. She got more tips that way, and the extra personal bargains that gave her the means to maintain her style of living. All her lovers had always accepted her living entirely free. For that made it possible for her to keep them living carefree and sweet.

Rose was disappointed in Jake. She had wanted him to live in the usual sweet way, to be brutal and beat her up a little, and take away her money from her. Once she had a rough leather-brown man who used to beat her up regularly. Sometimes she was beaten so badly she had to stay indoors for days, and to her visiting girl pals she exhibited her bruises and blackened eyes with pride.

As Jake was not brutally domineering, she cooled off from him perceptibly. But she could not make him change. She confided to her friends that he was "good loving but" (making use of a contraction that common people employ) "a big Ah-Ah all the same." She felt no thrill about the business when her lover was not interested in her earnings.

Jake did not care. He did not love her, had never felt any deep desire for her. He had gone to live with her simply because she had asked him when he was in a fever mood for a steady mate. There was nothing about Rose that touched and roused him as his vivid recollection of his charming little brown-skin of the Baltimore. Rose's room to him was like any ordinary lodging in Harlem. While the room of his little lost brown lived in his mind a highly magnified affair: a bed of gold, fresh, white linen, a magic carpet, all bathed in the rarest perfume. .. . Rose's perfume made his nose itch. It was rank.

He came home another afternoon and found her with a bright batik kimono carelessly wrapped around her and stretched full-length on the couch. There were Melachrino stubs lying about and his bottle of Scotch was on the mantelpiece. Evidently the strange visitor of the week before had been there again.

"Hello!" She yawned and flicked off her cigarette ash and continued smoking. A chic veneer over a hard, restless, insensitive body. Fascinating, nevertheless. . . . For the moment, just as she was, she was desirable and provoked responses in him. He shuffled up to the couch and caressed her.

"Leave me alone, I'm tired," she snarled.

The rebuff hurt Jake. "You slut!" he cried. He went over to the mantelpiece and added, "Youse just everybody's teaser."

"You got a nearve talking to me that way," said Rose. "Since when you staht riding the high horse?"

"It don't take no nearve foh me to tell you what you is. Fact is I'm right now sure tiahd to death of living with you."

"You poor black stiff!" Rose cried. And she leaped over at Jake and scratched at his face.

Jake gave her two savage slaps full in her face and she dropped moaning at his feet.

"There! You done begged foh it," he said. He stepped over her and went out.

Walking down the street, he looked at his palms. "Ahm shame o' you, hands," he murmured. "Mah mother useter tell me, 'Nevah hit no woman,' but that hussy jest made me do it . . . jest *made* me. . . . Well, I'd better pull outa that there mud-hole. . . . It wasn't what I come back to Gawd's own country foh. No, sirree! You bet it wasn't. . . ."

When he returned to the house he heard laughter in the room. Gertie Blake was there and Rose was telling a happy tale. He stood by the closed door and listened for a while.

"Have another drink, Gertie. Don't ever get a wee bit delicate when youse with me. . . . My, mah dear, but he did slap the daylights outa me. When I comed to I wanted to kiss his feet, but he was gone."

"Rose! You're the limit. But didn't it hurt awful?"

"Didn't hurt enough. Honey, it's the first time I ever felt his real strength. A hefty-looking one like him, always acting so nice and proper. I almost thought he was getting sissy. But he's a *ma-an* all right. . . ."

A nasty smile stole into Jake's features. He could not face those women. He left the house again. He strolled down to Dixie Red's pool-room and played awhile. From there he went with Zeddy to Uncle Doc's saloon.

He went home again and found Rose stunning in a new cloth-of-gold frock shining with brilliants. She was refixing a large artificial yellow rose to the side of a pearl-beaded green turban. Jake, without saying a word, went to the closet and took down his suitcase. Then he began tossing shirts, underwear, collars, and ties on to the couch.

"What the devil you're doing?" Rose wheeled round and stared at him in amazement, both hands gripping the dresser behind her.

"Kain't you see?" Jake replied.

She moved down on him like a panther, swinging her hips in a wonderful, rhythmical motion. She sprang upon his neck and brought him down.

"Oh, honey, you ain't mad at me 'counta the little fuss tonight?"

"I don't like hitting no womens," returned Jake's hard-breathing muffled voice.

"Daddy! I love you the more for that."

"You'll spile you' new clothes," Jake said, desperately.

"Hell with them! I love mah daddy moh'n anything. And mah daddy loves me, don't he? Daddy!"

Rose switched on the light and looked at her watch.

"My stars, daddy! We been honey-dreaming some! I am two hours late."

She jumped up and jig-stepped. "I should

worry if the Congo . . . I should worry mumbo-jumbo."

She smoothed out her frock, arranged her hair, and put the turban on. "Come along to the Congo a little later," she said to Jake. "Let's celebrate on champagne."

The door closed on him. . . .

"O Lawdy!" he yawned, stretched himself, and got up. He took the rest of his clothes out of the closet, picked up the crumpled things from the couch, packed, and walked out with his suitcase.

SECOND PART

SECOND PART

THE RAILROAD

X

*O*VER the heart of the vast gray Pennsylvania country the huge black animal snorted
and roared, with sounding rods and couplings,
pulling a long chain of dull-brown boxes
packed with people and things, trailing on the
blue-cold air its white masses of breath.

Hell was playing in the hot square hole of
a pantry and the coffin-shaped kitchen of the
dining-car. The short, stout, hard-and-horny
chef was terrible as a rhinoceros. Against the
second, third, and fourth cooks he bellied his
way up to the little serving door and glared at
the waiters. His tough, aproned front was a
challenge to them. In his oily, shining face
his big white eyes danced with meanness. All
the waiters had squeezed into the pantry at
once, excitedly snatching, dropping and
breaking things.

"Hey, you there! You mule!"[1] The chef shouted at the fourth waiter. "Who told you to snitch that theah lamb chops outa the hole?"

"I done think they was the one I ordered ——"

"Done think some hell, you down-home black fool. Ain't no thinking to be done on here ——"

"Chef, ain't them chops ready yet?" a waiter asked.

"Don't rush me, nigger," the chef bellowed back. "Wha' yu'all trying to do? Run me up a tree? Kain't run this here chef up no tree. Jump off ef you kain't ride him." His eyes gleamed with grim humor. "Jump off or lay down. This heah white man's train service ain't no nigger picnic."

The second cook passed up a platter of chops. The chef rushed it through the hole and licked his fingers.

"There you is, yaller. Take it away. Why ain't you gone yet? Show me some service,

---

[1] The fourth waiter on the railroad is nick-named "mule" because he works under the orders of the pantry-man.

yaller, show me some service." He rocked his thick, tough body sideways in a sort of dance, licked the sweat from his brow with his forefinger and grunted with aggressive self-satisfaction. Then he bellied his way back to the range and sent the third cook up to the serving window.

"Tha's the stuff to hand them niggers," he told the third cook. "Keep 'em up a tree all the time, but don't let 'em get you up there."

Jake, for he was the third cook, took his place by the window and handed out the orders. It was his first job on the railroad, but from the first day he managed his part perfectly. He rubbed smoothly along with the waiters by remaining himself and not trying to imitate the chef nor taking his malicious advice.

Jake had taken the job on the railroad just to break the hold that Harlem had upon him. When he quitted Rose he felt that he ought to get right out of the atmosphere of Harlem. If I don't git away from it for a while, it'll sure git me, he mused. But not ship-and-port-

town life again. I done had enough a that
here and ovah there. . . . So he had picked
the railroad. One or two nights a week in
Harlem. And all the days on the road. He
would go on like that until he grew tired of
that rhythm. . . .

The rush was over. Everything was quiet.
The corridors of the dining-car were emptied
of their jam of hungry, impatient guests. The
"mule" had scrubbed the slats of the pantry
and set them up to dry. The other waiters had
put away silver and glasses and soiled linen.
The steward at his end of the car was going
over the checks. Even the kitchen work was
finished and the four cooks had left their coffin
for the good air of the dining-room. They
sat apart from the dining-room boys. The
two grades, cooks and waiters, never chummed
together, except for gambling. Some of the
waiters were very haughty. There were certain light-skinned ones who went walking
with pals of their complexion only in the stop-
over cities. Others, among the older men,
were always dignified. They were fathers of

families, their wives moved in some sphere of
Harlem society, and their movements were
sometimes chronicled in the local Negro
newspapers.

Sitting at one of the large tables, four of the
waiters were playing poker. Jake wanted to
join them, but he had no money. One waiter
sat alone at a small table. He was reading.
He was of average size, slim, a smooth pure
ebony with straight features and a suggestion
of whiskers. Jake shuffled up to him and
asked him for the loan of two dollars. He
got it and went to play. . . .

Jake finished playing with five dollars. He
repaid the waiter and said: "Youse a good
sport. I'll always look out for you in that
theah hole."

The waiter smiled. He was very friendly.
Jake half-sprawled over the table. "Wha's
this here stuff you reading? Looks lak Greek
to me." He spelled the title, "S-A-P-H-O,
Sapho."

"What's it all about?" Jake demanded, flat-

tening down the book on the table with his
friendly paw. The waiter was reading the
scene between Fanny and Jean when the lover
discovers the letters of his mistress's former
woman friend and exclaims: "Ah *Oui* . . .
Sapho . . . *toute la lyre.* . . ."

"It's a story," he told Jake, "by a French
writer named Alphonse Daudet. It's about a
sporting woman who was beautiful like a rose
and had the soul of a wandering cat. Her
lovers called her Sapho. I like the story, but
I hate the use of Sapho for its title."

"Why does you?" Jake asked.

"Because Sappho was a real person. A
wonderful woman, a great Greek poet——"

"So theah *is* some Greek in the book!" said
Jake.

The waiter smiled. "In a sense, yes."

And he told Jake the story of Sappho, of
her poetry, of her loves and her passion for
the beautiful boy, Phaon. And of her leaping
into the sea from the Leucadian cliff because
of her love for him.

"Her story gave two lovely words to modern language," said the waiter.

"Which one them?" asked Jake.

"Sapphic and Lesbian . . . b e a u t i f u l words."

"What is that there Leshbian?"

". . . Lovely word, eh?"

"Tha's what we calls bulldyker in Harlem," drawled Jake. "Them's all ugly womens."

"Not *all*. And that's a damned ugly name," the waiter said. "Harlem is too savage about some things. *Bulldyker*," the waiter stressed with a sneer.

Jake grinned. "But tha's what they is, ain't it?"

He began humming:

"And there is two things in Harlem I don't understan'
It is a bulldyking woman and a faggoty man. . . ."

Charmingly, like a child that does not know its letters, Jake turned the pages of the novel. . . .

"Bumbole! This heah language is most different from how they talk it."

"Bumbole" was now a popular expletive for Jake, replacing such expressions as "Bull," "bawls," "walnuts," and "blimey." Ever since the night at the Congo when he heard the fighting West Indian girl cry, "I'll slap you bumbole," he had always used the word. When his friends asked him what it meant, he grinned and said, "Ask the monks."

"You know French?" the waiter asked.

"Parlee-vous? Mademoiselle, un baiser, s'il vous plait. Voilà! I larned that much offn the froggies."

"So you were over there?"

"Au oui, camarade," Jake beamed. "I was way, way ovah there after Democracy and them boches, and when I couldn't find one or the other, I jest turned mah black moon from the A. E. F. . . . But you! How come you jest plowing through this here stuff lak that? I could nevah see no light at all in them print, chappie. *Eh bien. Mais vous compris beaucoup."*

"C'est ma langue maternelle."

"Hm!" Jake made a face and scratched his

head. "*Comprendre pas,* chappie. Tell me in straight United States."

"French is my native language. I ——"

"Don't crap me," J a k e interrupted. "Ain'tchu—ain'tchu one of us, too?"

"Of course I'm Negro," the waiter said, "but I was born in Hayti and the language down there is French."

"Hayti . . . Hayti," r e p e a t e d Jake. "Tha's where now? Tha's ——"

"An island in the Caribbean—near the Panama Canal."

Jake sat like a big eager boy and learned many facts about Hayti before the train reached Pittsburgh. He learned that the universal spirit of the French Revolution had reached and lifted up the slaves far away in that remote island; that Black Hayti's independence was more dramatic and picturesque than the United States' independence and that it was a strange, almost unimaginable eruption of the beautiful ideas of the "Liberté, Egalité, Fraternité" of Mankind, that shook the foundations of that romantic era.

For the first time he heard the name Toussaint L'Ouverture, the black slave and leader of the Haytian slaves. Heard how he fought and conquered the slave-owners and then protected them; decreed laws for Hayti that held more of human wisdom and nobility than the Code Napoleon; defended his baby revolution against the Spanish and the English vultures; defeated Napoleon's punitive expedition; and how tragically he was captured by a civilized trick, taken to France, and sent by Napoleon to die broken-hearted in a cold dungeon.

"A black man! A black man! Oh, I wish I'd been a soldier under sich a man!" Jake said, simply.

He plied his instructor with questions. Heard of Dessalines, who carried on the fight begun by Toussaint L'Ouverture and kept Hayti independent. But it was incredible to Jake that a little island of freed slaves had withstood the three leading European powers. The waiter told him that Europe was in a complex state of transition then, and that that wonderful age had been electrified with universal ideas—ideas so big that they had lifted up ignorant people, even black, to the stature of gods.

"The world doesn't know," he continued, "how great Toussaint L'Ouverture really was. He was not merely great. He was lofty. He was good. The history of Hayti today might have been different if he had been allowed to finish his work. He was honored by a great enigmatic poet of that period. And I honor both Toussaint and the poet by keeping in my memory the wonderful, passionate lines."

He quoted Wordsworth's sonnet.

"Toussaint, the most unhappy Man of Men!
  Whether the whistling Rustic tend his plough
  Within thy hearing, or thy head be now
Pillowed in some deep dungeon's earless den;—
Oh miserable Chieftain! Where and when
  Wilt thou find patience? Yet die not; do thou
  Wear rather in thy bonds a cheerful brow:
Though fallen Thyself never to rise again,
Live, and take comfort. Thou hast left behind
  Powers that will work for thee, air, earth, and skies;
There's not a breathing of the common wind
  That will forget thee; thou hast great allies;

Thy friends are exultations, agonies,
And love, and Man's unconquerable Mind."

Jake felt like one passing through a dream, vivid in rich, varied colors. It was revelation beautiful in his mind. That brief account of an island of savage black people, who fought for collective liberty and was struggling to create a culture of their own. A romance of his race, just down there by Panama. How strange!

Jake was very American in spirit and shared a little of that comfortable Yankee contempt for poor foreigners. And as an American Negro he looked askew at foreign niggers. Africa was jungle, and Africans bush niggers, cannibals. And West Indians were monkey-chasers. But now he felt like a boy who stands with the map of the world in colors before him, and feels the wonder of the world.

The waiter told him that Africa was not jungle as he dreamed of it, nor slavery the peculiar rôle of black folk. The Jews were the slaves of the Egyptians, the Greeks made slaves of their conquered, the Gauls and Sax-

ons were slaves of the Romans. He told Jake
of the old destroyed cultures of West Africa
and of their vestiges, of black kings who struggled stoutly for the independence of their
kingdoms: Prempreh of Ashanti, Tofa of
Dahomey, Gbehanzin of Benin, Cetawayo of
Zulu-Land, Menelik of Abyssinia. . . .

Had Jake ever heard of the little Republic
of Liberia, founded by American Negroes?
And Abyssinia, deep-set in the shoulder of
Africa, besieged by the hungry wolves of
Europe? The only nation that has existed
free and independent from the earliest records
of history until today! Abyssinia, oldest un-
conquered nation, ancient-strange as Egypt,
persistent as Palestine, legendary as Greece,
magical as Persia.

There was the lovely legend of her queen
who visited the court of the Royal Rake of
Jerusalem, and how he fell in love with her.
And her beautiful black body made the Sage
so lyrical, he immortalized her in those wonderful pagan verses that are sacred to the
hearts of all lovers—even the heart of the

Church. . . . The catty ladies of the court of
Jerusalem were jealous of her. And Sheba reminded them that she was black but beautiful.
. . . And after a happy period she left Jerusalem and returned to her country with the
son that came of the royal affair. And that
son subsequently became King of Abyssinia.
And to this day the rulers of Abyssinia carry
the title, Lion of Judah, and trace their
descent direct from the liaison of the Queen of
Sheba with King Solomon.

First of Christian nations also is the claim
of this little kingdom! Christian since the
time when Philip, the disciple of Jesus, met
and baptized the minister of the Queen of
Abyssinia and he returned to his country and
converted the court and people to Christianity.

Jake listened, rapt, without a word of inter-
ruption.

"All the ancient countries have been yield-
ing up the buried secrets of their civili-
zations," the waiter said. "I wonder what
Abyssinia will yield in her time? Next to the
romance of Hayti, because it is my native

country, I should love to write the romance of
Abyssinia . . . Ethiopia."

"Is that theah country the same Ethiopia
that we done l'arned about in the Bible?"
asked Jake.

"The same. The Latin peoples still call it
Ethiopia."

"Is you a professor?"

"No, I'm a student."

"Whereat? Where did you l'arn English?"

"Well, I learned English home in Port-
au-Prince. And I was at Howard. You
know the Negro university at Washington.
Haven't even finished there yet."

"Then what in the name of mah holy rabbit foot youse doing on this heah white man's
chuh-chuh? It ain't no place foh no student.
It seems to me you' place down there sounds a
whole lot better."

"Uncle Sam put me here."

"Whadye mean Uncle Sam?" cried Jake.
"Don't hand me that bull."

"Let me tell you about it," the waiter said.
"Maybe you don't know that during the

[137]

World War Uncle Sam grabbed Hayti. My father was an official down there. He didn't want Uncle Sam in Hayti and he said so and said it loud. They told him to shut up and he wouldn't, so they shut him up in jail. My brother also made a noise and American marines killed him in the street. I had nobody to pay for me at the university, so I had to get out and work. *Voilà!*"

"And you ain't gwine to study no moh?"

"Never going to stop. I study now all the same when I get a little time. Every free day I have in New York I spend at the library downtown. I read there and I write."

Jake shook his head. "This heah work is all right for me, but for a chappie like you. . . . Do you like waiting on them ofays? 'Sall right working longshore or in a kitchen as I does it, but to be rubbing up against them and bowing so nice and all a that. . . ."

"It isn't so bad," the waiter said. "Most of them are pretty nice. Last trip I waited on a big Southern Senator. He was perfectly gentlemanly and tipped me half a dollar. When I have the blues I read Dr. Frank Crane."

Jake didn't understand, but he spat and said a stinking word. The chef called him to do something in the kitchen.

"Leave that theah professor and his nonsense," the chef said. . . .

The great black animal whistled sharply and puff-puffed slowly into the station of Pittsburgh.

SNOWSTORM IN PITTSBURGH

XI

*I*N THE middle of the little bridge built over the railroad crossing he was suddenly enveloped in a thick mass of smoke spouted out by an in-rushing train. That was Jake's first impression of Pittsburgh. He stepped off the bridge into a saloon. From there along a dull-gray street of grocery and fruit shops and piddling South-European children. Then he was on Wiley Avenue, the long, gray, uphill street.

Brawny bronze men in coal-blackened and oil-spotted blue overalls shadowed the doorways of saloons, pool-rooms, and little basement restaurants. The street was animated with dark figures going up, going down. Houses and men, women, and squinting cats and slinking dogs, everything seemed touched with soot and steel dust.

"So this heah is the niggers' run," said Jake.

"I don't like its 'pearance, nohow." He walked down the street and remarked a bouncing little chestnut-brown standing smartly in the entrance of a basement eating-joint. She wore a knee-length yellow-patterned muslin frock and a white-dotted blue apron. The apron was a little longer than the frock. Her sleeves were rolled up. Her arms were beautiful, like smooth burninshed bars of copper.

Jake stopped and said, "Howdy!"

"Howdy again!" the girl flashed a row of perfect teeth at him.

"Got a bite of anything good?"

"I should say so, Mister Ma-an."

She rolled her eyes and worked her hips into delightful free-and-easy motions. Jake went in. He was not hungry for food. He looked at a large dish half filled with tapioca pudding. He turned to the pie-case on the counter.

"The peach pie is the best," said the girl, her bare elbow on the counter; "it's fresh." She looked straight in his eyes. "All right,

I'll try peach," he said, and, magnetically, his
long, shining fingers touched her hand. . . .

In the evening he found the Haytian waiter
at the big Wiley Avenue pool-room. Quite
different from the pool-rooms in Harlem, it
was a sort of social center for the railroad men
and the more intelligent black workmen of the
quarter. Tobacco, stationery, and odds and
ends were sold in the front part of the store.
There was a table where customers sat and
wrote letters. And there were pretty chocolate dolls and pictures of Negroid types on
sale. Curious, pathetic pictures; black Ma-
donna and child; a kinky-haired mulatto
angel with African lips and Nordic nose, soaring on a white cloud up to heaven; Jesus bless-
ing a black child and a white one; a black
shepherd carrying a white lamb—all queerly
reminiscent of the crude prints of the great
Christian paintings that are so common in
poor religious homes.

"Here he is!" Jake greeted the waiter.
"What's the new?"

"Nothing new in Soot-hill; always the same."

The railroad men hated the Pittsburgh run. They hated the town, they hated Wiley Avenue and their wretched free quarters that were in it. . . .

"What're you going to do?"

"Ahm gwine to the colored show with a li'l' brown piece," said Jake.

"You find something already? My me! You're a fast-working one."

"Always the same whenever I hits a new town. Always in cock-tail luck, chappie."

"Which one? Manhattan or Bronx?"

"It's Harlem-Pittsburgh thisanight," Jake grinned. "Wachyu gwine make?"

"Don't know. There's nothing ever in Pittsburgh for me. I'm in no mood for the leg-show tonight, and the colored show is bum. Guess I'll go sleep if I can."

"Awright, I'll see you li'l' later, chappie." Jake gripped his hand. "Say—whyn't you tell a fellow you' name? Youse sure more'n

second waiter as Ise more'n third cook. Ev'-
body calls me Jake. And you?"

"Raymond, but everybody calls me Ray."

Jake heaved off. Ray bought some weekly
Negro newspapers: *The Pittsburgh Courier,
The Baltimore American, The Negro World,
The Chicago Defender.* Here he found a big
assortment of all the Negro publications that
he never could find in Harlem. In a next-
door saloon he drank a glass of sherry and
started off for the waiters' and cooks' quarters.

It was long after midnight when Jake returned to quarters. He had to pass through
the Western men's section to get to the Eastern
crews. Nobody was asleep in the Western
men's section. No early-morning train was
chalked up on their board. The men were
grouped off in poker and dice games. Jake
hesitated a little by one group, fascinated by a
wiry little long-headed finger-snapping black,
who with strenuous h'h, h'h, h'h, h'h, was zest-
fully throwing the bones. Jake almost joined
the game but he admonished himself: "You
winned five dollars thisaday and you made a

nice li'l' brown piece. Wha'more you
want?" . . .

He found the beds assigned to the members
of his crew. They were double beds, like
Pullman berths. Three of the waiters had not
come in yet. The second and the fourth cooks
were snoring, each a deep frothy bass and a
high tenor, and scratching themselves in their
sleep. The chef sprawled like the carcass of a
rhinoceros, half-naked, mouth wide open.
Tormented by bedbugs, he had scratched and
tossed in his sleep and hoofed the covers off
the bed. Ray was sitting on a lower berth on
his Negro newspapers spread out to form a
sheet. He had thrown the sheets on the floor,
they were so filthy from other men's sleeping.
By the thin flame of gaslight he was killing
bugs.

"Where is I gwine to sleep?" asked Jake.

"Over me, if you can. I saved the bunk for
you," said Ray.

"Some music the niggers am making," remarked Jake, nodding in the direction of the

snoring cooks. "But whasmat, chappie, you ain't sleeping?"

"Can't you see?"

"Bugs. Bumbole! This is a hell of a dump for a man to sleep in."

"The place is rocking crazy with them," said Ray. "I hauled the cot away from the wall, but the mattress is just swarming."

Hungry and bold, the bugs crept out of their chinks and hunted for food. They stopped dead-still when disturbed by the slightest shadow, and flattened their bellies against the wall.

"Le's get outa this stinking dump and chase a drink, chappie."

Ray jumped out of his berth, shoved himself into his clothes and went with Jake. The saloon near by the pool-room was still open. They went there. Ray asked for sherry.

"You had better sample some hard liquor if youse gwine back to wrastle with them bugs tonight," Jake suggested.

Ray took his advice. A light-yellow fellow chummed up with the boys and invited them to drink with him. He was as tall as Jake and very thin. There was a vacant, wandering look in his, kindly-weak eyes. He was a waiter on another dining-car of the New York-Pittsburg run. Ray mentioned that he had to quit his bed because he couldn't sleep.

"This here town is the rottenest lay-over in the whole railroad field," declared the light-yellow. "I don't never sleep in the quarters here."

"Where do you sleep, then?" asked Ray.

"Oh, I got a sweet baby way up yonder the other side of the hill."

"Oh, ma-ma!" Jake licked his lips. "So youse all fixed up in this heah town?"

"Not going there tonight, though," the light-yellow said in a careless, almost bored tone. "Too far for mine."

He asked Jake and Ray if they would like to go to a little open-all-night place. They were glad to hear of that.

"Any old thing, boh," Jake said, "to get away from that theah Pennsy bug house."

The little place was something of a barrel-house speak-easy, crowded with black steel-workers in overalls and railroad men, and foggy with smoke. They were all drinking hard liquor and playing cards. The boss was a stocky, genial brown man. He knew the light-yellow waiter and shook hands with him and his friends. He moved away some boxes in a corner and squeezed a little table in it, specially for them. They sat down, jammed into the corner, and drank whisky.

"Better here than the Pennsy pigpen," said the light-yellow.

He was slapped on the back by a short, compact young black.

"Hello, you! What you think youse doing theah?"

"Ain't figuring," retorted the light-yellow, "is you?"

"On the red moon gwine around mah haid, yes. How about a li'l' good snow?"

"Now you got mah number down, Happy."

The black lad vanished again through a mysterious back door.

[148]

The light-yellow said: "He's the biggest hophead I ever seen. Nobody can sniff like him. Yet he's always the same happy nigger, stout and strong like a bull."

He took another whisky and went like a lean hound after Happy. Jake looked mischievously at the little brown door, remarking: "It's a great life ef youse in on it." . . .

The light-yellow came back with a cold gleam in his eyes, like arsenic shining in the dark. His features were accentuated by a rigid, disturbing tone and he resembled a smiling wax figure.

"Have a li'l' stuff with the bunch?" he asked Jake.

"I ain't got the habit, boh, but I'll try anything once again."

"And you?" The light-yellow turned to Ray.

"No, chief, thank you, but I don't want to."

The waiter went out again with Jake on his heels. Beyond the door, five fellows, kneeling in the sawdust, were rolling the square bones.

[149]

Others sat together around two tables with a bottle of red liquor and thimble-like glasses before them.

"Oh, boy!" one said. "When I get home tonight it will be some more royal stuff. I ain'ta gwine to work none 'tall tomorrow."

"Shucks!" Another spread away his big mouth. "This heah ain't nothing foh a fellow to turn royal loose on. I remimber when I was gwine with a money gang that hed no use foh nothing but the pipe. That theah time was life, buddy."

"Wha' sorta pipe was that there?" asked Jake.

"The Chinese stuff, old boy."

Instead of deliberately fisting his, like the others, Jake took it up carelessly between his thumb and forefinger and inhaled.

"Say what you wanta about Chinee or any other stuff," said Happy, "but theah ain't nothing can work wicked like snow and whisky. It'll flip you up from hell into heaven befoh you knows it."

Ray looked into the room.

"Who's you li'l' mascot?" Happy asked the light-yellow.

"Tha's mah best pal," Jake answered. "He's got some moh stuff up here," Jake tapped his head.

"Better let's go on back to quarters," said Ray.

"To them bugs?" demanded Jake.

"Yes, I think we'd better."

"Awright, anything you say, chappie. I kain sleep through worser things." Jake took a few of the little white packets from Happy and gave him some money. "Guess I might need them some day. You never know."

Jake fell asleep as soon as his head touched the dirty pillow. Below him, Ray lay in his bunk, tormented by bugs and the snoring cooks. The low-burning gaslight flickered and flared upon the shadows. The young man lay under the untellable horror of a dead-tired man who wills to sleep and cannot.

In other sections of the big barn building

the faint chink of coins touched his ears. Those men gambling the hopeless Pittsburg night away did not disturb him. They were so quiet. It would have been better, perhaps, if they were noisy. He closed his eyes and tried to hynotize himself to sleep. Sleep . . . sleep . . . sleep . . . sleep . . . sleep. . . . He began counting slowly. His vigil might break and vanish somnolently upon some magic number. He counted a million. Perhaps love would appease this unwavering angel of wakefulness. Oh, but he could not pick up love easily on the street as Jake. . . .

He flung himself, across void and water, back home. Home thoughts, if you can make them soft and sweet and misty-beautiful enough, can sometimes snare sleep. There was the quiet, chalky-dusty street and, jutting out over it, the front of the house that he had lived in. The high staircase built on the outside, and pots of begonias and ferns on the landing. . . .

All the flowering things he loved, red and white and pink hibiscus, mimosas, rhododendrons, a thousand glowing creepers, climbing and spilling their vivid petals everywhere, and bright-buzzing humming-birds and butterflies. All the tropic-warm lilies and roses. Giddy-high erect thatch palms, slender, tall, fur-fronded ferns, majestic cotton trees, stately bamboos creating a green grandeur in the heart of space. . . .

Sleep remained cold and distant. Intermittently the cooks broke their snoring with masticating noises of their fat lips, like animals eating. Ray fixed his eyes on the offensive bug-bitten bulk of the chef. These men claimed kinship with him. They were black like him. Man and nature had put them in the same race. He ought to love them and feel them (if they felt anything). He ought to if he had a shred of social morality in him. They were all chain-ganged together and he was counted as one link. Yet he loathed every soul in that great barrack-room, except Jake. Race. . . . Why should he have and love a race?

Races and nations were things like skunks,

whose smells poisoned the air of life. Yet civilized mankind reposed its faith and future in their ancient, silted channels. Great races and big nations! There must be something mighty inspiriting in being the citizen of a great strong nation. To be the white citizen of a nation that can say bold, challenging things like a strong man. Something very different from the keen ecstatic joy a man feels in the romance of being black. Something the black man could never feel nor quite understand.

Ray felt that as he was conscious of being black and impotent, so, correspondingly, each marine down in Hayti must be conscious of being white and powerful. What a unique feeling of confidence about life the typical white youth of his age must have! Knowing that his skin-color was a passport to glory, making him one with ten thousands like himself. All perfect Occidentals and investors in that grand business called civilization. That grand business in whose pits sweated and snored, like the cooks, all the black and brown

[154]

hybrids and mongrels, simple earth-loving animals, without aspirations toward national unity and racial arrogance.

He remembered when little Hayti was floundering uncontrolled, how proud he was to be the son of a free nation. He used to feel condescendingly sorry for those poor African natives; superior to ten millions of suppressed Yankee "coons." Now he was just one of them and he hated them for being one of them. . . .

But he was not entirely of them, he reflected. He possessed another language and literature that they knew not of. And some day Uncle Sam might let go of his island and he would escape from the clutches of that magnificent monster of civilization and retire behind the natural defenses of his island, where the steam-roller of progress could not reach him. Escape he would. He had faith. He had hope. But, oh, what would become of that great mass of black swine, hunted and cornered by slavering white canaille! Sleep! oh, sleep! Down Thought!

But all his senses were burning wide awake.

[155]

Thought was not a beautiful and reassuring angel, a thing of soothing music and light laughter and winged images glowing with the rare colors of life. No. It was suffering, horribly real. It seized and worried him from every angle. Pushed him toward the sheer precipice of imagination. It was awful. He was afraid. For thought was a terrible tiger clawing at his small portion of gray substance, throttling, tearing, and tormenting him with pitiless ferocity. Oh, a thousand ideas of life were shrieking at him in a wild orgy of mockery! . . .

He was in the middle of a world suspended in space. A familiar line lit up, like a flame, the vast, crowded, immensity of his vision.

Et l'âme du monde est dans l'air.

A moment's respite. . . .

A loud snore from the half-naked chef brought him back to the filthy fact of the quarters that the richest railroad in the world had provided for its black servitors. Ray looked up at Jake, stretched at full length on his side, his cheek in his right hand, sleeping peacefully, like a tired boy after hard playing, so happy and sweet and handsome. He remembered the neatly-folded white papers in Jake's pocket. Maybe that was the cause of his sleeping so soundly. He reached his hand up to the coat hanging on the nail above his head. It was such an innocent little thing—like a headache powder the paper of which you wipe with your tongue, so that none should be wasted. Apparently the first one had no effect and Ray took the rest.

Sleep capitulated.

Immediately he was back home again. His father's house was a vast forest full of blooming hibiscus and mimosas and giant evergreen trees. And he was a gay humming-bird, fluttering and darting his long needle beak into the heart of a bell-flower. Suddenly he changed into an owl flying by day. . . . Howard University was a prison with white warders. . . . Now he was a young shining chief in a marble palace; slim, naked ne-

gresses dancing for his pleasure; courtiers re-
clining on cushions soft like passionate kisses;
gleaming-skinned black boys bearing goblets
of wine and obedient eunuchs waiting in the
offing. . . .

And the world was a blue paradise. Everything was in gorgeous blue of heaven. Woods
and streams were blue, and men and women
and animals, and beautiful to see and love.
And he was a blue bird in flight and a blue
lizard in love. And life was all blue happiness. Taboos and terrors and penalties were
transformed into new pagan delights, orgies
of Orient-blue carnival, of rare flowers and
red fruits, cherubs and seraphs and fetishes
and phalli and all the most-high gods. . . .

A thousand pins were pricking Ray's flesh
and he was shouting for Jake, but his voice
was so faint he could not hear himself. Jake
had him in his arms and tried to stand him
upon his feet. He crumpled up against the
bunk. All his muscles were loose, his cells
were cold, and the rhythm of being arrested.

It was high morning and time to go to the

train. Jake had picked up the empty little folds of paper from the floor and restored them to his pocket. He knew what had happened to them, and guessed why. He went and called the first and fourth waiters.

The chef bulked big in the room, dressed and ready to go to the railroad yards. He gave a contemptuous glance at Jake looking after Ray and said: "Better leave that theah nigger professor alone and come on 'long to the dining-car with us. That theah nigger is dopey from them books o' hisn. I done told befoh them books would git him yet."

The chef went off with the second and fourth cooks. Jake stayed with Ray. They got his shoes and coat on. The first waiter telephoned the steward, and Ray was taken to the hospital.

"We may all be niggers aw'right, but we ain't nonetall all the same," Jake said as he hurried along to the dining-car, thinking of Ray.

XII

*P*ERHAPS the chef of Jake's dining-car was the most hated chef in the service. He was repulsive in every aspect. From the elevated bulk of his gross person to the matted burrs of his head and the fat cigar, the constant companion of his sloppy mouth, that he chewed and smoked at the same time. The chef deliberately increased his repulsiveness of form by the meannesses of his spirit.

"I know Ise a mean black nigger," he often said, "and I'll let you all know it on this heah white man's car, too."

The chef was a great black bundle of consciously suppressed desires. That was doubtless why he was so ornery. He was one of the model chefs of the service. His kitchen was well-ordered. The checking up of his provisions always showed a praiseworthy balance. He always had his food ready on time, feeding the heaviest rush of customers as rapidly as the lightest. He fed the steward excellently. He fed the crew well. In a word, he did his duty as only a martinet can.

A chef who is "right-there" at every call is the first asset of importance on an *à la carte* restaurant-car. The chef lived rigidly up to that fact and above it. He was also painfully honest. He had a mulatto wife and a brown boy-child in New York and he never slipped away any of the company's goods to them. Other dining-car men had devised a system of getting by the company's detectives with choice brands of the company's foodstuffs. The chef kept away from that. It was long since the yard detectives had stopped searching any parcel that *he* carried off with him.

"I don't want none o' the white-boss stuff foh mine," he declared. "Ise making enough o' mah own to suppoht mah wife and kid."

And more, the chef had a violent distaste for all the stock things that "coons" are supposed to like to the point of stealing them. He would not eat watermelon, because white

people called it "the niggers' ice-cream."
Pork chops he fancied not. Nor corn pone.
And the idea of eating chicken gave him a
spasm. Of the odds and ends of chicken gizzard, feet, head, rump, heart, wing points, and
liver—the chef would make the most delicious
stew for the crew, which he never touched
himself. The Irish steward never missed his
share of it. But for his meal the chef would
grill a steak or mutton chop or fry a fish. Oh,
chef was big and haughty about not being "no
regular darky"! And although he came from
the Alabama country, he pretended not to
know a coon tail from a rabbit foot.

"All this heah talk about chicken-loving
niggers," he growled chuckingly to the second
cook. "The way them white passengers clean
up on mah fried chicken I wouldn't trust one
o' them anywheres near mah hen-coop."

Broiling tender corn-fed chicken without
biting a leg. Thus, grimly, the chef existed.
Humored and tolerated by the steward and
hated by the waiters and undercooks. Jake

found himself on the side of the waiters. He did not hate the chef (Jake could not hate anybody). But he could not be obscenely sycophantic to him as the second cook, who was just waiting for the chance to get the chef's job. Jake stood his corner in the coffin, doing his bit in diplomatic silence. Let the chef bawl the waiters out. He would not, like the second cook, join him in that game.

Ray, perhaps, was the chief cause of Jake's silent indignation. Jake had said to him: "I don't know how all you fellows can stand that theah God-damn black bull. I feels like falling down mahself." But Ray had begged Jake to stay on, telling him that he was the only decent man in the kitchen. Jake stayed because he liked Ray. A big friendship had sprung up between them and Jake hated to hear the chef abusing his friend along with the other waiters. The other cooks and waiters called Ray "Professor." Jake had never called him that. Nor did he call him "buddy," as he did Zeddy and his longshore-

men friends. He called him "chappie" in a
genial, semi-paternal way.

Jake's life had never before touched any of
the educated of the ten dark millions. He
had, however, a vague idea of who they were.
He knew that the "big niggers" that were gossiped about in the saloons and the types he had
met at Madame Adelina Suarez's were not
the educated ones. The educated "dick-tees,"
in Jake's circles were often subjects for raw
and funny sallies. He had once heard Miss
Curdy putting them in their place while
Susy's star eyes gleamed warm approval.

"Honey, I lived in Washington and I
knowed inside and naked out the stuck-up
bush-whackers of the race. They all talks and
act as if loving was a sin, but I tell you
straight, I wouldn't trust any of them after
dark with a preacher. . . . Don't ask me,
honey. I seen and I knows them all."

"I guess you does, sistah," Susy had agreed.
"Nobody kaint hand *me* no fairy tales about
niggers. Wese all much of a muchness when
you git down to the real stuff."

Difficulties on the dining-car were worsened by a feud between the pantry and the kitchen. The first waiter, who was pantryman by regulation, had a grievance against the chef and was just waiting to "get" him. But, the chef being such a paragon, the "getting" was not easy.

Nothing can be worse on a dining-car than trouble between the pantry and the kitchen, for one is as necessary to the other as oil is to salad. But the war was covertly on and the chef was prepared to throw his whole rhinoceros weight against the pantry. The first waiter had to fight cautiously. He was quite aware that a first-class chef was of greater value than a first-class pantryman.

The trouble had begun through the "mule." The fourth man—a coffee-skinned Georgia village boy, timid like a country girl just come to town—hated the nickname, but the chef would call him nothing else.

"Call him 'Rhinoceros' when he calls you

'Mule,' " Ray told the fourth waiter, but he was too timid to do it. . . .

The dining-car was resting on the tracks in the Altoona yards, waiting for a Western train. The first, third, and fifth waiters were playing poker. Ray was reading Dostoievski's *Crime and Punishment*. The fourth waiter was working in the pantry. Suddenly the restaurant-car was shocked by a terrible roar.

"Gwan I say! Take that theah ice and beat it, you black sissy." . . .

"This ice ain't good for the pantry. You ought to gimme the cleaner one," the timid fourth man stood his ground.

The cigar of the chef stood up like a tusk. Fury was dancing in his enraged face and he would have stamped the guts out of the poor, timid boy if he was not restrained by the fear of losing his job. For on the dining-car, he who strikes the first blow catches the punishment.

"Quit jawing with me, nigger waiter, or I'll jab this heah ice-pick in you' mouf."

"Come and do it," the fourth waiter said, quietly.

"God dam' you' soul!" the chef bellowed. "Ef you don't quit chewing the rag—ef you git fresh with me, I'll throw you off this bloody car. S'elp mah Gawd, I will. You disnificant down-home mule."

The fourth waiter glanced behind him down the corridor and saw Ray, book in hand, and the other waiters, who had left their cards to see the cause of the tumult. Ray winked at the fourth waiter. He screwed up his courage and said to the chef: "I ain't no mule, and youse a dirty rhinoceros."

The chef seemed paralyzed with surprise. "Wha's that name you done call me? Wha's rhinasras?"

All the waiters laughed. The chef looked ridiculous and Ray said: "Why, chef, don't you know? That's the ugliest animal in all Africa."

The chef looked apoplectic. . . . "I don't care a dime foh all you nigger waiters and I ain't joking wif any of you. Cause you manicuring you' finger nails and rubbing up you' stinking black hide against white folks in that theah diner, you all think youse something. But lemme tell you straight, you ain't nothing atall."

"But, chef," cried the pantryman, "why don't you stop riding the fourth man? Youse always riding him."

"Riding who? I nevah rode a man in all mah life. I jest tell that black skunk what to do and him stahts jawing with me. I don't care about any of you niggers, nohow."

"Wese all tiahd of you cussin' and bawking," said the pantryman. "Why didn't you give the boy a clean piece of ice and finish? You know we need it for the water."

"Yaller nigger, you'd better gwan away from here."

"Don't call me no yaller nigger, you black and ugly cotton-field coon."

"Who dat? You bastard-begotten dime-snatcher, you'd better gwan back to you' dining-room or I'll throw this heah garbage in you' crap-yaller face. . . . I'd better git long

far away from you all 'foh I lose mah haid."
The chef bounced into the kitchen and
slammed the door.

That "bastard-begotten dime-snatcher"
grew a cancer in the heart of the pantryman.
It rooted deep because he *was* an "illegiti-
mate" and he bitterly hated the whites he
served ("crackers," he called them all) and
the tips he picked up. He knew that his
father was some red-necked white man who
had despised his mother's race and had done
nothing for him.

The sight of the chef grew more and more
unbearable each day to the pantryman. He
thought of knifing or plugging him with a
gun some night. He had nursed his resent-
ment to the point of madness and was capable
of any act. But getting the chef in the dark
would not have been revenge enough. The
pantryman wanted the paragon to live, so that
he might invent a way of bringing him down
humiliatingly from his perch.

But the chef was hard to "get." He had
made and kept his place by being a perfect

brutal machine, with that advantage that all mechanical creatures have over sensitive human beings. One day the pantryman thought he almost had his man. The chef had fed the steward, but kept the boys waiting for their luncheon. The waiters thought that he had one of his ornery spells on and was intentionally punishing them. They were all standing in the pantry, except Ray.

The fifth said to the first: "Ask him why he don't put the grub in the hole, partner. I'm horse-ways hungry."

"Ask him you'self. I ain't got nothing to do with that black hog moh'n giving him what b'longs to him in this heah pantry."

"Mah belly's making a most beautiful commotion. Jest lak a bleating lamb," drawled the third.

The fifth waiter pushed up the little glass door and stuck his head in the kitchen: "Chef, when are we gwine to go away from here?"

"Keep you' shirt on, nigger," flashed back from the kitchen. "Youall'll soon be stuffing you'self full o' the white man's poke chops. Better than you evah smell in Harlem."

"Wese werking foh't same like you is," the fifth man retorted.

"I don't eat no poke chops, nigger. I cooks the stuff, but I don't eat it, nevah."

"P'raps youse chewing a worser kind o' meat."

"Don't gimme no back talk, nigger waiter. Looka heah ——"

The steward came into the pantry and said: "Chef, it's time to feed the boys. They're hungry. We had a hard day, today."

The chef's cigar drooped upon his slavering lip and almost fell. He turned to the steward with an injured air. "Ain't I doing mah best? Ain't I been working most hard mahself? I done get yourn lunch ready and am getting the crew's own and fixing foh dinner at the same time. I ain't tuk a mouful mahse'f ——"

The steward had turned his heels on the pantry. The chef was enraged that he had intervened on behalf of the waiters.

"Ef you dime-chasing niggers keep fooling

with me on this car," he said, "I'll make you
eat mah spittle. I done do it a'ready and I'll
do it again. I'll spit in you' eats ———"

"Wha's that? The boss sure gwine to settle
this." The pantryman dashed out of the
pantry and called the steward. . . . "Ain't
any of us waiters gwine to stay on heah Mis'r
Farrel, with a chef like this."

"What's that, now?" The steward was in
the pantry again. "What's this fine story,
chef?"

"Nothing at all, Sah Farrel. I done pull a
good bull on them fellars, tha's all. Cause
theyse all trying to get mah goat. L'em quit
fooling with the kitchen, Sah Farrel. I does
mah wuk and I don't want no fooling fwom
them nigger waiters, nohow."

"I guess you spit in it as you said, all right,"
cried the pantryman. . . . "Yes, you! You'd
wallow in a pigpen and eat the filth, youse so
doggone low-down."

"Now cut all o' that out," said the steward.
"How could he do anything like that, when
he eats the food, and I do meself?"

[172]

"In the hole!" shouted Jake.

The third and fifth waiters hurried into the pantry and brought out the waiters' food. . . . First a great platter of fish and tomatoes, then pork chops and mashed potatoes, steaming Java and best Borden's cream. The chef had made home-made bread baked in the form of little round caps. Nice and hot, they quickly melted the butter that the boys sandwiched between them. He was a splendid cook, an artist in creating palatable stuff. He came out of the kitchen himself, to eat in the dining-room and, diplomatically, he helped himself from the waiters' platter of fish. . . . Delicious food. The waiters fell to it with keen relish. Obliterated from their memory the sewer-incident of the moment before. . . . Feeding, feeding, feeding.

But Ray remembered and visualized, and his stomach turned. He left the food and went outside, where he found Jake taking the air. He told Jake how he felt.

"Oh, the food is all right," said Jake. "I watch him close anough in that there kitchen, and he knows I ain't standing in with him in no low-down stuff."

"But do you think he would ever do such a thing?" asked Ray.

Jake laughed. "What won't a bad nigger do when he's good and mean way down in his heart? I ain't 'lowing mahself careless with none o' that kind, chappie."

Two Pullman porters came into the dining-car in the middle of the waiters' meal.

"Here is the chambermaids," grinned the second cook.

"H'm, but how you all loves to call people names, though," commented the fourth waiter.

The waiters invited the porters to eat with them. The pantryman went to get them coffee and cream. The chef offered to scramble some eggs. He went back to the kitchen and, after a few minutes, the fourth cook brought out a platter of scrambled eggs for the two porters. The chef came rocking importantly behind the fourth cook. A clean white cap was poised on his head and fondly he chewed his cigar. A perfect menial of the great railroad company. He felt a wave of goodness sweeping over him, as if he had been patted on the head by the Angel Gabriel for his good works. He asked the porters if they had enough to eat and they thanked him and said they had more than enough and that the food was wonderful. The chef smiled broadly. He beamed upon steward, waiters, and porters, and his eyes said: See what a really fine fellow I am in spite of all the worries that go with the duties of a chef?

One day Ray saw the chef and the pantryman jesting while the pantryman was lighting his cigarette from the chef's stump of cigar. When Ray found the pantryman alone, he laughingly asked him if he and the chef had smoked the tobacco of peace.

"Fat chance!" retorted the first waiter. "I gotta talk to him, for we get the stores together and check up together with the steward, and I gotta hand him the stuff tha's coming to him outa the pantry, but I ain't settle mah debt with him yet. I ain't got no time for no nigger that done calls me 'bastard-begotten' and means it."

"Oh, forget it!" said Ray. "Christ was one, too, and we all worship him."

"Wha' you mean?" the pantryman demanded.

"What I said," Ray replied. . . .

"Oh! . . . Ain't you got no religion in you none 'tall?"

"My parents were Catholic, but I ain't nothing. God is white and has no more time for niggers than you've got for the chef."

"Well, I'll be browned but once!" cried the pantryman. "Is that theah what youse l'arning in them books? Don't you believe in getting religion?"

Ray laughed.

"You kain laugh, all right, but watch you' step Gawd don't get you yet. Youse sure trifling."

The coldness between the kitchen and the pantry continued, unpleasantly nasty, like the wearing of wet clothes, after the fall of a heavy shower, when the sun is shining again. The chef was uncomfortable. A waiter had never yet opposed open hostility to his personality like that. He was accustomed to the crew's surrendering to his ways with even a little sycophancy. It was always his policy to be amicable with the pantryman, playing him against the other waiters, for it was very disagreeable to keep up a feud when the kitchen and the pantry had so many unavoidable close contacts.

So the chef made overtures to the pantryman with special toothsome tidbits, such as he always prepared for the only steward and himself. But the pantryman refused to have any specially-prepared-for-his-Irishness-the-Steward's stuff that the other waiters could not share. Thereupon the chef gave up trying to placate him and started in hating back with profound African hate. African hate is deep down and hard to stir up, but there is no hate more realistic when it is stirred up.

One morning in Washington the iceman forgot to supply ice to the dining-car. One of the men had brought a little brass top on the diner and the waiters were excited over an easy new game called "put-and-take." The pantryman forgot his business. The chef went to another dining-car and obtained ice for the kitchen. The pantryman did not remember anything about ice until the train was well on its way to New York. He remembered it because the ice-cream was turning soft. He put his head through the hole and asked Jake for a piece of ice. The chef said no, he had enough for the kitchen only.

With a terrible contented expression the chef looked with malicious hate into the pantryman's yellow face. The pantryman glared back at the villainous black face and jerked his head in rage. The ice-cream turned softer. . . .

Luncheon was over, all the work was done, everything in order, and the entire crew was ready to go home when the train reached New York. The steward wanted to go directly home. But he had to wait and go over to the yards with the keys, so that the pantryman could ice up. And the pantryman was severely reprimanded for his laxity in Washington. . . .

The pantryman bided his time, waiting on the chef. He was cordial. He even laughed at the jokes the chef made at the other waiters' expense. The chef swelled bigger in his hide, feeling that everything had bent to his will. The pantryman waited, ignoring little moments for the big moment. It came.

One morning both the second and the fourth cook "fell down on the job," neither of them reporting for duty. The steward placed an order with the commissary superintendent for two cooks. Jake stayed in the kitchen, working, while the chef and the pantryman went to the store for the stock. . . .

The chef and the pantryman returned together with the large baskets of provisions for the trip. The eggs were carried by the chef himself in a neat box. Remembering that he had forgotten coffee, he sent Jake back to the store for it. Then he began putting away the kitchen stuff. The pantryman was putting away the pantry stuff. . . .

A yellow girl passed by and waved a smile at the chef. He grinned, his teeth champing his cigar. The chef hated yellow men with "cracker" hatred, but he loved yellow women with "cracker" love. His other love was gin. But he never carried a liquor flask on the diner, because it was against regulations. And he never drank with any of the crew. He drank alone. And he did other things alone. In Philadelphia or Washington he never went to a buffet flat with any of the men.

The girls working in the yards were always flirting with him. He fascinated them, perhaps because he was so Congo mask-like in aspect and so duty-strict. They could often wheedle something nice out of other chefs, but nothing out of *the* chef. He would rather give them his money than a piece of the company's raw meat. The chef was generous in his way; Richmond Pete, who owned the saloon near the yards in Queensborough, could attest to that. He had often gossiped about the chef. How he "blowed them gals that he had a crush on in the family room and danced an elephant jig while the gals were pulling his leg."

The yellow girl that waved at the chef through the window was pretty. Her gesture transformed his face into a foolish broad-smiling thing. He stepped outside the kitchen for a moment to have a tickling word with her.

In that moment the pantryman made a lightning-bolt move; and shut down the little glass door between the pantry and the kitchen. . . .

The train was speeding its way west. The first call for dinner had been made and the dining-room was already full. Over half a dozen calls for eggs of different kinds had been bawled out before the chef discovered that the basket of eggs was missing. The chef asked the pantryman to call the steward. The pantryman, curiously preoccupied, forgot. Pandemonium was loose in the pantry and kitchen when the steward, radish-red, stuck his head in.

The chef's lower lip had flopped low down, dripping, and the cigar had fallen somewhere. "Cut them aiggs off o' the bill, Sah Farrel. O Lawd!" he moaned, "Ise sartain sure I brought them aiggs on the car mahself, and now I don't know where they is."

"What kind o' blah is that?" cried the steward. "The eggs must be there in the kitchen. I saw them with the stock meself."

"And I brought them here hugging them, Boss, ef I ain't been made fool of by something." The rhinoceros had changed into a meek black lamb. "O Lawd! and I ain't been outa the kitchen sence. Ain't no mortal hand could tuk them. Some evil hand. O Lawd!——"

"Hell!" The steward dashed out of the

pantry to cut all the egg dishes off the bill. The passengers were getting clamorous. The waiters were asking those who had ordered eggs to change to something else. . . .

The steward suggested searching the pantry. The pantry was ransacked. "Them ain't there, cep'n' they had feets to walk. O Lawd of Heaben!" the chef groaned. "It's something deep and evil, I knows, for I ain't been outa this heah kitchen." His little flirtation with the yellow girl was completely wiped off his memory.

Only Jake was keeping his head in the kitchen. He was acting second cook, for the steward had not succeeded in getting one. The fourth cook he had gotten was new to the service and he was standing, conspicuously long-headed, with gaping mouth.

"Why'n the debbil's name don't you do some'n, nigger?" bellowed the chef, frothy at the corners of his mouth.

"The chef is up a tree, all right," said Ray to the pantryman.

"And he'll break his black hide getting down," the pantryman replied, bitterly.

"Chef!" The yellow pantryman's face carried a royal African grin. "What's the matter with you and them aiggs?"

"I done gived them to you mammy."

"And fohget you wife, ole timer? Ef you ain't a chicken-roost nigger, as you boast, you surely loves the nest."

Gash! The chef, at last losing control of himself, shied a huge ham bone at the pantryman. The pantryman sprang back as the ham bone flew through the aperture and smashed a bottle of milk in the pantry.

"What's all this bloody business today?" cried the steward, who was just entering the pantry. . . . "What nonsense is this, chef? You've made a mess of things already and now you start fighting with the waiters. You can't do like that. You losing your head?"

"Lookahere, Sah Farrel, I jes' want ev'body to leave me 'lone."

"But we must all team together on the dining-car. That's the only way. You can't start fighting the waiters because you've lost the eggs."

"Sah Farrel, leave me alone, I say," half roared, half moaned the chef, "or I'll jump off right now and let you run you' kitchen you'-self."

"What's that?" The steward started.

"I say I'll jump off, and I mean it as Gawd's mah maker."

The steward slipped out of the pantry without another word.

The steward obtained a supply of eggs in Harrisburg the next morning. The rest of the trip was made with the most dignified formalities between him and the chef. Between the pantry and the chef the atmosphere was tenser, but there were no more explosions.

The dining-car went out on its next trip with a new chef. And the old chef, after standing a little of the superintendent's notoriously sharp tongue, was sent to another car as second cook.

"Hit those fellahs in the pocket-book is the only way," the pantryman overheard the steward talking to one of his colleagues. "Imagine an old experienced chef threatening to jump off when I was short of a second cook."

They were getting the stock for the next trip in the commissary. Jake turned to the pantryman: "But it was sure peculiar, though, how them aiggs just fly outa that kitchen lak that way."

"Maybe they all hatched and growed wings when ole black bull was playing with that sweet yaller piece," the pantryman laughed.

"Honest, though, how do you think it happened?" persisted Jake. "Did you hoodoo them aiggs, or what did you do?"

"I wouldn't know atall. Better ask them rats in the yards ef they sucked the shells dry. What you' right hand does don't tell it to the left, says I."

"You done said a mou'ful, but how did you get away with it so quiet?"

"I ain't said nothing discrimination and I ain't nevah."

"Don't figure against me. Ise with you, buddy," said Jake, "and now that wese good and rid of him, I hope all we niggers will pull together like civilization folks."

"Sure we will. There ain't another down-home nigger like him in this white man's serv-ice. He was riding too high and fly, brother. I knew he would tumble and bust something nasty. But I ain't said I knowed a thing about it, all the same."

XIII

ONE night in Philadelphia Jake breezed into the waiters' quarters in Market Street, looking for Ray. It was late. Ray was in bed. Jake pulled him up.

"Come on outa that, you slacker. Let's go over to North Philly."

"What for?"

"A li'l' fun. I knows a swell outfit I wanta show you."

"Anything new?"

"Don't know about anything *new,* chappie, but I know there's something *good* right there in Fifteenth Street."

"Oh, I know all about that. I don't want to go."

"Come on. Don't be so particular about you' person. You gotta go with me."

"I have a girl in New York."

"Tha's awright. This is Philly."

"I tell you, Jake, there's no fun in those kinds for me. They'll bore me just like that night in Baltimore."

"Oh, these here am different chippies, I tell you. Come on, le's spend the night away from this damn dump. Wese laying ovah all day tomorrow."

"And some of them will say such rotten things. Pretty enough, all right, but their mouths are loaded with filth, and that's what gets me."

"Them's different ovah there, chappie. I'll kiss the Bible on it. Come on, now. It's no fun me going alone."

They went to a house in Fifteenth Street. As they entered Jake was greeted by a mulatto woman in the full vigor of middle life.

"Why, *you* heart-breaker! It's ages and ages since I saw you. You and me sure going to have a bust-up tonight."

Jake grinned, prancing a little, as if he were going to do the old cake-walk.

[189]

"Here, Laura, this is mah friend," he introduced Ray casually.

"Bring him over here and sit down," Madame Laura commanded.

She was a big-boned woman, but very agile. A long, irregular, rich-brown face, roving black eyes, deep-set, and shiny black hair heaped upon her head. She wore black velvet, a square-cut blouse low down on her breasts, and a string of large coral beads. The young girls of that house envied her finely-preserved form and her carriage and wondered if they would be anything like that when they reached her age.

The interior of this house gave Ray a shock. It looked so much like a comfortable boarding-house where everybody was cheerful and nice coquettish girls in colorful frocks were doing the waiting. . . . There were a few flirting couples, two groups of men playing cards, and girls hovering around. An attractive black woman was serving sandwiches, gin and bottled beer. At the piano, a slim yellow youth was playing a "blues." . . . A pleasant house party, similar to any other among colored people of that class in Baltimore, New Orleans, Charleston, Richmond, or even Washington, D. C. Different, naturally, from New York, which molds all peoples into a hectic rhythm of its own. Yet even New York, passing its strange thousands through its great metropolitan mill, cannot rob Negroes of their native color and laughter.

"Mah friend's just keeping me company," Jake said to the woman. "He ain't regular—you get me? And I want him treated right."

"He'll be treated better here than he would in church." She laughed and touched Ray's calf with the point of her slipper.

"What kind o' bust-up youse gwine to have with me?" demanded Jake.

"I'll show you just what I'm going to do with you for forgetting me so long."

She got up and went into an adjoining room. When she returned an attractively made-up brown girl followed her carrying a tray with glasses and a bottle of champagne.

. . . The cork hit the ceiling, bang! And deftly the woman herself poured the foaming liquor without a wasted drop.

"There! That's our bust-up," she said. "Me and you and your friend. Even if he's a virgin he's all right. I know you ain't never going around with no sap-head."

"Give me some, too," a boy of dull-gold complexion materialized by the side of Madame Laura and demanded a drink. He was about eleven years old.

Affectionately she put her arm around him and poured out a small glass of champagne. The frailness of the boy was pathetic; his eyes were sleepy-sad. He resembled a reed fading in a morass.

"Who is he?" Ray asked.

"He's my son," responded Madame Laura. "Clever kid, too. He loves books."

"Ray will like him, then," said Jake. "Books is his middle name."

Ray suddenly felt a violent dislike for the atmosphere. At first he had liked the general friendliness and warmth and naturalness of it.

All so different from what he had expected.
But something about the presence of the little
boy there and his being the woman's son disgusted him. He could not analyse his aver-
sion. It was just an instinctive, intolerant
feeling that the boy did not belong to that environment and should not be there.

He went from Madame Laura and Jake
over to the piano and conversed with the pianist. When he glanced again at the table he
had left, Madame Laura had her arm around
Jake's neck and his eyes were strangely
shining.

Madame Laura had set the pace. There
were four other couples making love. At one
table a big-built, very black man was amusing
himself with two attractive girls, one brown-
skinned and the other yellow. The girls' complexion was heightened by High-Brown Talc
powder and rouge. A bottle of Muscatel
stood on the table. The man was well
dressed in nigger-brown and he wore an expensive diamond ring on his little finger.

The stags were still playing cards, with

girls hovering over them. The happy-faced
black woman was doing the managing, as Madame Laura was otherwise engaged. The
pianist began banging another blues.

Ray felt alone and a little sorry for himself.
Now that he was there, he would like to be
touched by the spirit of that atmosphere and,
like Jake, fall naturally into its rhythm. He
also envied Jake. Just for this night only he
would like to be like him. . . .

They were dancing. The little yellow girl,
her legs kicked out at oblique angles, appeared
as if she were going to fall through the big-
built black man.

> We'll all be merry when you taste a cherry,
> And we'll twine and twine like a fruitful vine.

In the middle of the floor, a young railroad
porter had his hand flattened straight down
the slim, cérise-chiffoned back of a brown girl.
Her head was thrown back and her eyes held
his gleaming eyes. Her lips were parted with
pleasure and they stood and rocked in an

ecstasy. Their feet were not moving. Only their bodies rocked, rocked to the "blues." . . .

Ray remarked that Jake was not in the room, nor was Madame Laura in evidence. A girl came to him. "Why is you so all by you'self, baby? Don't you wanta dance some? That there is some more temptation 'blues.'"

Tickling, enticing syncopation. Ray felt that he ought to dance to it. But some strange thing seemed to hold him back from taking the girl in his arms.

"Will you drink something, instead?" he found a way out.

"Awwww-right," d i s a p p o i n t e d , she drawled.

She beckoned to the happy-faced woman.

"Virginia Dare."

"I'll have some, too," Ray said.

Another brown girl joined them.

"Buy mah pal a drink, too?" the first girl asked.

"Why, certainly," he answered.

The woman brought two glasses of Virginia Dare and Ray ordered a third.

Such a striking exotic appearance the rouge gave these brown girls. Rouge that is so cheap in its general use had here an uncommon quality. Rare as the red flower of the hibiscus would be in a florist's window on Fifth Avenue. Rouge on brown, a warm, insidious chestnut color. But so much more subtle than chestnut. The round face of the first girl, the carnal sympathy of her full, tinted mouth, touched Ray. But something was between them. . . .

The piano-player had wandered off into some dim, far-away, ancestral source of music. Far, far away from music-hall syncopation and jazz, he was lost in some sensual dream of his own. No tortures, banal shrieks and agonies. Tum-tum . . . tum-tum . . . tum-tum . . . tum-tum. . . . The n o t e s were naked acute alert. Like black youth burning naked in the bush. Love in the deep heart of the jungle. . . . The sharp spring of a leopard from a leafy limb, the snarl of a jackal, green lizards in amorous play, the flight of a plumed bird, and the sudden laugh-

ter of mischievous monkeys in their green
homes. Tum-tum . . . tum-tum . . . tum-
tum . . . tum-tum. . . . Simple-clear a n d
quivering. Like a primitive dance of war or
of love . . . the marshaling of spears or the
sacred frenzy of a phallic celebration.

Black lovers of life caught up in their own
free native rhythm, threaded to a remote
scarce-remembered past, celebrating the midnight hours in themselves, for themselves, of
themselves, in a house in Fifteenth Street,
Philadelphia. . . .

"Raided!" A voice screamed. Standing in
the rear door, a policeman, white, in full uniform, smilingly contemplated the spectacle.
There was a wild scramble for hats and wraps.
The old-timers giggled, shrugged, and kept
their seats. Madame Laura pushed aside the
policeman.

"Keep you' pants on, all of you and carry
on with you' fun. What's matter? Scared of
a uniform? Pat"—she turned to the policeman—"what you want to throw a scare in the
company for? Come on here with you."

The policeman, twirling his baton, marched to a table and sat down with Madame Laura.

"Geewizard!" Jake sat down, too. "Tell 'em next time not to ring the fire alarm so loud."

"You said it, honey-stick. There are no cops in Philly going to mess with this girl. Ain't it the truth, Pat?" Madame Laura twisted the policeman's ear and bridled.

"I know it's the Bible trute," the happy-faced black lady chanted in a sugary voice, setting a bottle of champagne and glasses upon the table and seating herself familiarly beside the policeman.

The champagne foamed in the four glasses.

"Whar's mah li'l' chappie?" Jake asked.

"Gone, maybe. Don't worry," said Madame Laura. "Drink!"

Four brown hands and one white. Chink!

"Here's to you, Pat," cried Madame Laura. "There's Irish in me from the male line." She toasted:

"Flixy, flaxy, fleasy,
  Make it good and easy,

[198]

Flix for start and flax for snappy,
Niggers and Irish will always be happy."

The policeman swallowed his champagne at a gulp and got up. "Gotta go now. Time for duty."

"You treat him nice. Is it for love or protection?" asked Jake.

"He's loving *her*"—Madame Laura indicated the now coy lady who helped her manage—"but he's protecting *me*. It's a long time since I ain't got no loving inclination for any skin but chocolate. Get me?"

When Jake returned to the quarters he found Ray sleeping quietly. He did not disturb him. The next morning they walked together to the yards.

"Did the policeman scare you, too, last night?" asked Jake.

"What policeman?"

"Oh, didn't you see him? There was a policeman theah and somebody hollered 'Raid!' scaring everybody. I thought you'd done tuk you'self away from there in quick time becasn a that."

"No, I left before that, I guess. Didn't even smell one walking all the way to the quarters in Market Street."

"Why'd you beat it? One o' the li'l' chippies had a crush on you. Oh, boy! and she was some piece to look at."

"I know it. She was kind of nice. But she had some nasty perfume on her that turned mah stomach."

"Youse awful queer, chappie," Jake commented.

"Why, don't you ever feel those sensations that just turn you back in on yourself and make you isolated and helpless?"

"Wha'd y'u mean?"

"I mean if sometimes you don't feel as I felt last night?"

"Lawdy no. Young and pretty is all I feel."

They stopped in a saloon. Jake had a small whisky and Ray an egg-nogg.

"But Madame Laura isn't young," resumed Ray.

"Ain't she?" Jake showed his teeth. "I'd back her against some of the youngest. She's a wonder, chappie. Her blood's like good liquor. She gave me a present, too. Looka here." Jake took from his pocket a lovely slate-colored necktie sprinkled with red dots. Ray felt the fineness of it.

"Ef I had the sweetman disinclination I wouldn't have to work, chappie," Jake rocked proudly in his walk. "But tha's the life of a pee-wee cutter, says I. Kain't see it for mine."

"She was certainly nice to you last night. And the girls were nice, too. It was just like a jolly parlor social."

"Oh, sure! Them gals not all in the straight business, you know. Some o' them works and just go there for a good time, a li'l' extra stuff. . . . It ain't like that nonetall ovah in Europe, chappie. They wouldn't 'a' treated you so nice. Them places I sampled ovah there was all straight raw business and no camoflage."

"Did you prefer them?"

"Hell, no! I prefer the niggers' way every time. They does it better. . . ."

"Wish I could feel the difference as you do, Jakie. I lump all those ladies together, without difference of race."

"Youse crazy, chappie. You ain't got no experience about it. There's all kinds a difference in that theah life. Sometimes it's the people make the difference and sometimes it's the place. And as foh them sweet marchants, there's as much difference between them as you find in any other class a people. There is them slap-up private-apartmant ones, and there is them of the dickty buffet flats; then the low-down speakeasy customers; the cabaret babies, the family-entrance clients, and the street fliers."

They stopped on a board-walk. The dining-car stood before them, resting on one of the hundred tracks of the great Philadelphia yards.

"I got a free permit to a nifty apartmant in New York, chappie, and the next Saturday night we lay over together in the big city Ise gwine to show you some real queens. It's like everything else in life. Depends on you' luck."

"And you are one lucky dog," Ray laughed.

Jake grinned: "I'd tell you about a li'l' piece o' sweetness I picked up in a cabaret the first day I landed from ovah the other side. But it's too late now. We gotta start work."

"Next time, then," said Ray.

Jake swung himself up by the rear platform and entered the kitchen. Ray passed round by the other side into the dining-room.

XIV

*D*USK gathered in blue patches over the Black Belt. Lenox Avenue was vivid. The saloons were bright, crowded with drinking men jammed tight around the bars, treating one another and telling the incidents of the day. Longshoremen in overalls with hooks, Pullman porters holding their bags, waiters, elevator boys. Liquor-rich laughter, banana-ripe laughter. . . .

The pavement was a dim warm bustle. Women hurrying home from day's work to get dinner ready for husbands who worked at night. On their arms brown bags and black containing a bit of meat, a head of lettuce, butter. Young men who were stagging through life, passing along with brown-paper packages, containing a small steak, a pork chop, to do their own frying.

From out of saloons came the savory smell

of corned beef and cabbage, spare-ribs, Hamburger steaks. Out of little cook-joints wedged in side streets, tripe, pigs' feet, hogs' ears and snouts. Out of apartments, steak smothered with onions, liver and bacon, fried chicken.

The composite smell of cooked stuff assaulted Jake's nostrils. He was hungry. His landlady was late bringing his food. Maybe she was out on Lenox Avenue chewing the rag with some other Ebenezer soul, thought Jake.

Jake was ill. The doctor told him that he would get well very quickly if he remained quietly in bed for a few days.

"And you mustn't drink till you are better. It's bad for you," the doctor warned him.

But Jake had his landlady bring him from two to four pails of beer every day. "I must drink some'n," he reasoned, "and beer can't make me no harm. It's light."

When Ray went to see him, Jake laughed at his serious mien.

"Tha's life, chappie. I goes way ovah yonder and wander and fools around and I hed

no mind about nothing. Then I come back
to mah own home town and, oh, you snake-
bite! When I was in the army, chappie, they
useter give us all sorts o' lechers about can-
shankerous nights and prophet-lactic days, but
I nevah pay them no mind. Them things foh
edjucated guys like you who lives in you'
head."

"They are for you, too," Ray said. "This
is a new age with new methods of living. You
can't just go on like a crazy ram goat as if
you were living in the Middle Ages."

"Middle Ages! I ain't seen them yet and
don't nevah wanta. All them things you talk
about am kill-joy things, chappie. The trute
is they make me feel shame."

Ray laughed until tears trickled down his
cheeks. . . . He visualized Jake b e i n g
ashamed and laughed again.

"Sure," said Jake. "I'd feel ashame' ef a
chippie—No, chappie, them stuff is foh you
book fellahs. I runs around all right, but Ise
lak a sailor that don't know nothing about

using a compass, but him always hits a safe port."

"You didn't this time, though, Jakie. Those devices that you despise are really for you rather than for me or people like me, who don't live your kind of free life. If you, and the whole strong race of workingman who live freely like you, don't pay some attention to them, then you'll all wither away and rot like weeds."

"Let us pray!" said Jake.

"That I don't believe in."

"Awright, then, chappie."

On the next trip, the dining-car was shifted off its scheduled run and returned to New York on the second day, late at night. It was ordered out again early the next day. Ray could not get round to see Jake, so he telephoned his girl and asked her to go.

Agatha had heard much of Ray's best friend, but she had never met him. Men working on a train have something of the spirit of men working on a ship. They are,

[207]

perforce, bound together in comradeship of a
sort in that close atmosphere. In the stop-
over cities they go about in pairs or groups.
But the camaraderie breaks up on the platform in New York as soon as the dining-car
returns there. Every man goes his own way
unknown to his comrades. Wife or sweet-
heart or some other magnet of the great magic
city draws each off separately.

Agatha was a rich-brown girl, with soft
amorous eyes. She worked as assistant in a
beauty parlor of the Belt. She was a Baltimore girl and had been living in New York
for two years. Ray had met her the year
before at a basket-ball match and dance.

She went to see Jake in the afternoon. He
was sitting in a Morris chair, reading the
Negro newspaper, *The Amsterdam* News,
with a pail of beer beside him, when Agatha
rapped on the door.

Jake thought it was the landlady. He was
thrown off his balance by the straight, beautiful girl who entered the room and quietly
closed the door behind her.

"Oh, keep your seat, please," she begged him. "I'll sit there," she indicated a brown chair by the cherrywood chiffonier.

"Ray asked me to come. He was doubled out this morning and couldn't get around to see you. I brought these for you."

She put a paper bag of oranges on the table. "Where shall I put these?" She showed him a charming little bouquet of violets. Jake's drinking-glass was on the floor, half full, beside the pail of beer.

"It's all right, here!" On the chipped, mildew-white wash-stand there was another glass with a tooth-brush. She took the tooth-brush out, poured some water in the glass, put the violets in, and set it on the chiffonier.

"There!" she said.

Jake thanked her. He was diffident. She was so different a girl from the many he had known. She was certainly one of those that Miss Curdy would have sneered at. She was so full of simple self-assurance and charm. Mah little sister down home in Petersburg, he thought, might have turned out something

[209]

lak this ef she'd 'a' had a chance to talk English like in books and wear class-top clothes.
Nine years sence I quite home. She must be
quite a li'l' woman now herself.

Jake loved women's pretty clothes. The
plain nigger-brown coat Agatha wore, unbut-
toned, showed a fresh peach-colored frock.
He asked after Ray.

"I didn't see him myself this trip," she said.
"He telephoned me about you."

Jake praised Ray as his best pal.

"He's a good boy," she agreed. She asked
Jake about the railroad. "It must be lots of
fun to ride from one town to the other like
that. I'd love it, for I love to travel. But
Ray hates it."

"It ain't so much fun when youse working,"
replied Jake.

"I guess you're right. But there's something marvelous about meeting people for a
little while and serving them and never seeing
them again. It's romantic. You don't have
that awful personal everyday contact that do-
mestic workers have to get along with. If I

was a man and had to be in service, I wouldn't
want better than the railroad."

"Some'n to that, yes," agreed Jake. . . .
"But it ain't all peaches, neither, when all
them passengers rush you like a herd of hungry swine."

Agatha stayed twenty minutes.

"I wish you better soon," she said, bidding
Jake good-by. "It was nice to know you.
Ray will surely come to see you when he gets
back this time."

Jake drank a glass of beer and eased his
back, full length on the little bed.

"She is sure some wonderful brown," he
mused. "Now I sure does understand why
Ray is so scornful of them easy ones." He
gazed at the gray door. It seemed a shining
panel of gold through which a radiant vision
had passed.

"She sure does like that theah Ray an un-
conscionable lot. I could see the love stuff
shining in them mahvelous eyes of hers when
I talked about him. I s'pose it's killing sweet
to have some'n loving you up thataway.

Some'n real fond o' you for you own self lak, lak—jest lak how mah mammy useter love pa and do everything foh him bafore he done took and died off without giving no notice. . . . "

His thoughts wandered away back to his mysterious little brown of the Baltimore. She was not elegant and educated, but she was nice. Maybe if he found her again—it would be better than just running wild around like that! Thinking honestly about it, after all, he was never satisfied, flopping here and sleeping there. It gave him a little cocky pleasure to brag of his conquests to the fellows around the bar. But after all the swilling and boasting, it would be a thousand times nicer to have a little brown woman of his own to whom he could go home and be his simple self with. Lay his curly head between her brown breasts and be fondled and be the spoiled child that every man loves sometimes to be when he is all alone with a woman. *That* he could never be with the Madame Lauras. They expected him always to be the prancing he-man. Maybe it was the lack of a steady girl that kept him running crazy around. Boozing and poking and rooting around, jolly enough all right, but not altogether contented.

The landlady did not appear with Jake's dinner.

"Guess she is somewhere rocking soft with gin," he thought. "Ise feeling all right enough to go out, anyhow. Guess I'll drop in at Uncle Doc's and have a good feed of spare-ribs. Hm! but the stuff coming out of these heah Harlem kitchens is enough to knock me down. They smell so good."

He dressed and went out. "Oh, Lenox Avenue, but you look good to me, now. Lawdy! though, how the brown-skin babies am humping it along! Strutting the joy-stuff! Invitation for a shimmy. O Lawdy! Pills and pisen, you gotta turn me loose, quick."

Billy Biasse was drinking at the bar of Uncle Doc's when Jake entered.

"Come on, you, and have a drink," Billy cried. "Which hole in Harlem youse been burying you'self in all this time?"

"Which you figure? There is holes out-side of Harlem too, boh." Jake ordered a beer.

"Beer!" exclaimed Billy. "Quit you fool-ing and take some real liquor, nigger. Ise paying foh it. Order that theah ovah-water liquor you useter be so dippy about. That theah Scotch."

"I ain't quite all right, Billy. Gotta go slow on the booze."

"Whasmat? . . . Oh, foh Gawd's sake! Don't let the li'l' beauty break you' heart. Fix her up with gin."

"Might as well, and then a royal feed o' spare-ribs," agreed Jake.

He asked for Zeddy.

"Missing sence all the new moon done bless mah luck that you is, too. Last news I heard 'bout him, the gen'man was Yonkers an-chored."

"And Strawberry Lips?"

"That nigger's back home in Harlem where he belongs. He done long ago quit that ugly yaller razor-back. And you, boh. Who's providing foh you' wants sence you done turn Congo Rose down?"

"Been running wild in the paddock of the Pennsy."

"Oh, boh, you sure did breaks the sweet-loving haht of Congo Rose. One night she stahted to sing 'You broke mah haht and went away' and she jest bust out crying theah in the cabaret and couldn't sing no moh. She hauled harself whimpering out there, and she laid off o' the Congo foh moh than a week. That li'l' goosey boy had to do the strutting all by himse'f."

"She was hot stuff all right." Jake laughed richly. "But I had to quit her or she would have made me either a no-'count or a bad nigger."

Warmed up by meeting an old pal and hearing all the intimate news of the dives, Jake tossed off he knew not how many gins. He told Billy Biasse of the places he had nosed out in Baltimore and Philadelphia. The gossip was good. Jake changed to Scotch and asked for the siphon.

He had finished the first Scotch and asked for another, when a pain gripped his belly with a wrench that almost tore him apart. Jake groaned and doubled over, staggered into a corner, and crumpled up on the floor. Perspiration stood in beads on his forehead, trickled down his rigid, chiseled features. He heard the word "ambulance" repeated several times. He thought first of his mother. His sister. The little frame house in Petersburg. The backyard of bleached clothes on the line, the large lilac tree and the little forked lot that yielded red tomatoes and green peas in spring.

"No hospital foh me," he muttered. "Mah room is jest next doh. Take me theah."

Uncle Doc told his bar man to help Billy Biasse lift Jake.

"Kain you move you' laigs any at all, boh?" Billy asked.

Jake groaned: "I kain try."

The men took him home. . . .

[216]

Jake's landlady had been invited to a fried-chicken feed in the basement lodging of an Ebenezer sister and friend on Fifth Avenue. The sister friend had rented the basement of the old-fashioned house and appropriated the large backyard for her laundry work. She went out and collected soiled linen every Monday. Her wealthiest patrons sent their chauffeurs round with their linen. And the laundress was very proud of white chauffeurs standing their automobiles in front of her humble basement. She noticed with heaving chest that the female residents of the block rubber-necked. Her vocation was very profitable. And it was her pleasure sometimes to invite a sister of her church to dinner. . . .

The fried chicken, with sweet potatoes, was excellent. Over it the sisters chinned and ginned, recounting all the contemporary scandals of the Negro churches. . . .

At last Jake's landlady remembered him and staggered home to prepare his beef broth. But when she took it up to him she found that Jake was out. Returning to the kitchen, she

[217]

stumbled and broke the white bowl, made a sign with her rabbit foot, and murmured, foggily: "Theah's sure a cross coming to thisa house. I wonder it's foh who?"

The bell rang and rang again and again in spite of the notice: Ring once. And when the landlady opened the door and saw Jake supported between two men, she knew that the broken white bowl was for him and that his time was come.

XV

*B*ILLY BIASSE telephoned to the doctor, a young chocolate-complexioned man. He was graduate of a Negro medical college in Tennessee and of Columbia University. He was struggling to overcome the prejudices of the black populace against Negro doctors and wedge himself in among the Jewish doctors that prescribed for the Harlem clientele. A clever man, he was trying, through Democratic influence, to get an appointment in one of the New York hospitals. Such an achievement would put him all over the Negro press and get him all the practice and more than he could handle in the Belt.

Ray had sent Jake to him. . . .

The landlady brought Jake a rum punch. He shook his head. With a premonition of tragedy, she waited for the doctor, standing against the chiffonier, a blue cloth carelessly knotted round her head. . . .

In the corridor she questioned Billy Biasse about Jake's seizure.

"All you younger generation in Harlem don't know no God," she accused Billy and indicted Young Harlem. "All you know is cabarets and movies and the young gals them exposing them legs a theirs in them jumper frocks."

"I wouldn't know 'bout that," said Billy.

"You all ought to know, though, and think of God Almighty before the trumpet sound and it's too late foh black sinners. I nevah seen so many trifling and ungodly niggers as there is in this heah Harlem." She thought of the broken white bowl. "And I done had a warning from heaben."

The doctor arrived. Ordered a hot-water bottle for Jake's belly and a hot lemon drink. There was no other remedy to help him but what he had been taking.

"You've been drinking," the doctor said.

"Jest a li'l' beer," Jake murmured.

"O Lawdy! though, listen at him!" cried the landlady. "Mister, if he done had a glass, he had a barrel a day. Ain't I been getting it foh him?"

"Beer is the worst form of alcohol you could ever take in your state," said the doctor. "Couldn't be anything worse. Better you had taken wine."

Jake growled that he didn't like wine.

"It's up to you to get well," said the doctor. "You have been ill like that before. It's a simple affair if you will be careful and quiet for a little while. But it's very dangerous if you are foolish. I know you chaps take those things lightly. But you shouldn't, for the consequences are very dangerous."

Two days later Ray's diner returned to New York. It was early afternoon and the crew went over to the yards to get the stock for the next trip. And after stocking up Ray went directly to see Jake.

Jake was getting along all right again. But Ray was alarmed when he heard of his relapse. Indeed, Ray was too easily moved for the world he lived in. The delicate-fibered mechanism of his being responded to sensations that were entirely beyond Jake's comprehension.

"The doctor done hand me his. The landlady stahted warning me against sin with her mouth stinking with gin. And now mah chappie's gwina join the gang." Jake laughed heartily.

"But you must be careful, Jake. You're too sensible not to know good advice from bad."

"Oh, sure, chappie, I'll take care. I don't wanta be crippled up as the doctor says I might. Mah laigs got many moh miles to run yet, chasing after the sweet stuff o' life, chappie."

"Good oh Jake! I know you love life too much to make a fool of yourself like so many of those other fellows. I've never knew that this thing was so common until I started working on the railroad. You know the fourth had to lay off this trip."

"You don't say!"

"Yes, he's got a mean one. And the second cook on Bowman's diner he's been in a chronic way for about three months."

"But how does he get by the doctor? All them crews is examined every week."

"Hm! . . ." Ray glanced carelessly through *The Amsterdam News.* "I saw Madame Laura in Fairmount Park and I told her you were sick. I gave her your address, too."

"Bumbole! What for?"

"Because she asked me for it. She was sympathetic."

"I never give mah address to them womens, chappie. Bad system that."

"Why?"

"Because you nevah know when they might bust in on you and staht a rough-house. Them's all right, them womens . . . in their own parlors."

"I guess you ought to know. I don't," said Ray. "Say, why don't you move out of this dump up to the Forties? There's a room in the same house I stay in. Cheap. Two flights

up, right on the court. Steam heat and everything."

"I guess I could stand a new place to lay
mah carcass in, all right," Jake drawled.
"Steam heats you say? I'm sure sick o' this
here praying-ma-ma hot air. And the trute
is it ain't nevah much hotter than mah breath."

"All right. When do you want me to speak
to the landlady about the room?"

"This heah very beautiful night, chappie.
Mah rent is up tomorrow and I moves. But
you got to do me a li'l' favor. Go by Billy
Biasse this night and tell him to come and git
his ole buddy's suitcase and see him into his
new home tomorrow morning."

Jake was as happy as a kid. He would be
frisking if he could. But Ray was not happy.
The sudden upset of affairs in his home country had landed him into the quivering heart of
a naked world whose reality was hitherto unimaginable. It was what they called in print
and polite conversation "the underworld."
The compound word baffled him, as some
English words did sometimes. Why *under-*

world he could never understand. It was very much upon the surface as were the others divisions of human life. Having its heights and middle and depths and secret places even as they. And the people of this world, waiters, cooks, chauffeurs, sailors, porters, guides, ushers, hod-carriers, factory hands — all touched in a thousand ways the people of the other divisions. They worked over there and slept over here, divided by a street.

Ray had always dreamed of writing words some day. Weaving words to make romance, ah! There were the great books that dominated the bright dreaming and dark brooding days when he was a boy. *Les Misérables, Nana, Uncle Tom's Cabin, David Copperfield, Nicholas Nickleby, Oliver Twist.*

From them, by way of free-thought pamphlets, it was only a stride to the great scintillating satirists of the age—Bernard Shaw, Ibsen, Anatole France, and the popular problemist, H. G. Wells. He had lived on that brilliant manna that fell like a flame-fall from those burning stars. Then came the great mass carnage in Europe and the great mass revolution in Russia.

Ray was not prophetic-minded enough to define the total evil that the one had wrought nor the ultimate splendor of the other. But, in spite of the general tumults and threats, the perfectly-organized national rages, the ineffectual patching of broken, and hectic rebuilding of shattered, things, he had perception enough to realize that he had lived over the end of an era.

And also he realized that his spiritual masters had not crossed with him into the new. He felt alone, hurt, neglected, cheated, almost naked. But he was a savage, even though he was a sensitive one, and did not mind nakedness. What had happened? Had they refused to come or had he left them behind? Something had happened. But it was not desertion nor young insurgency. It was death. Even as the last scion of a famous line prances out this day and dies and is set aside with his ancestors in their cold whited sepulcher, so had his masters marched with flags and ban-

ners flying all their wonderful, trenchant, critical, satirical, mind-sharpening, pity-evoking,
constructive ideas of ultimate social righteous-
ness, into the vast international cemetery of
this century.

Dreams of patterns of words achieving
form. What would he ever do with the words
he had acquired? Were they adequate to tell
the thoughts he felt, describe the impressions
that reached him vividly? What were men
making of words now? During the war he
had been startled by James Joyce in *The Little Review*. Sherwood Anderson had reached
him with *Winesburg, Ohio*. He had read,
fascinated, all that D. H. Lawrence published. And wondered if there was not a great
Lawrence reservoir of words too terrible and
too terrifying for nice printing. Henri Bar-
busse's *Le Feu* burnt like a flame in his memory. Ray loved the book because it was such
a grand anti-romantic presentation of mind
and behavior in that hell-pit of life. And
literature, story-telling, had little interest for

him now if thought and feeling did not wrestle and sprawl with appetite and dark desire all over the pages.

Dreams of making something with words. What could he make . . . and fashion? Could he ever create Art? Art, around which vague, incomprehensible words and phrases stormed? What was art, anyway? Was it more than a clear-cut presentation of a vivid impression of life? Only the Russians of the late era seemed to stand up like giants in the new. Gogol, Dostoievski, Tolstoy, Chekhov, Turgeniev. When he read them now he thought: Here were elements that the grand carnage swept over and touched not. The soil of life saved their roots from the fire. They were so saturated, so deep-down rooted in it.

Thank God and Uncle Sam that the old dreams were shattered. Nevertheless, he still felt more than ever the utter blinding nakedness and violent coloring of life. But what of it? Could he create out of the fertile reality around him? Of Jake nosing through life, a handsome hound, quick to snap up any tempting morsel of poisoned meat thrown carelessly on the pavement? Of a work pal he had visited in the venereal ward of Bellevue, where youths lolled sadly about? And the misery that overwhelmed him there, until life appeared like one big disease and the world a vast hospital?

A PRACTICAL PRANK

XVI

MY DEAR HONEY-STICK

"I was riding in Fairmount Park one afternoon, just taking the air as usual, when I saw your proper-speaking friend with a mess of books. He told me you were sick and I was so mortïfied for I am giving a big evening soon and was all set on fixing it on a night when you would certain sure be laying over in Philadelphia. Because you are such good company I may as well say how much you are appreciated here. I guess I'll put it off till you are okay again, for as I am putting my hand in my own pocket to give all of my friends and wellwishers a dandy time it won't be no fun for *me* if I leave out the *principal* one. Guess who!

"I am expecting to come to New York soon on shopping bent. You know all us weak women who can afford it have got the Fifth Avenue fever, my dear. If I come I'll sure look you up, you can bank on it.

"Bye, bye, honeystick and be good and quiet and better yourself soon. Philadelphia is lonesome without you.

"Lovingly, LAURA."

Billy Biasse, calling by Jake's former lodging, found this letter for him, lying there among a pile of others, on the little black round table in the hall. . . .

"Here you is, boh. Whether youse well or sick, them's after you."

"Is they? Lemme see. Hm . . . Philly." . . .

"Who is you' pen-pusher?" asked Billy.

"A queen in Philly. Says she might pay me a visit here. I ain't send out no invitation foh no womens yet."

"Is she the goods?"

"She's a wang, boh. Queen o' Philly, I tell you. And foh me, everything with her is f. o. c. But I don't want that yaller piece o' business come nosing after me here in Harlem."

"She ain't got to find you, boh. Jest throws her a bad lead."

"Tha's the stuff to give 'm. Ain't you a buddy with a haid on, though?"

" 'Deed I is. And all you niggers knows it who done frequent mah place."

And so Jake, in a prankish mood, replied to Madame Laura on a picture post-card saying he would be well and up soon and be back on the road and on the job again, and he gave Congo Rose's address.

Madame Laura made her expected trip to New York, traveling "Chair," as was her custom when she traveled. She wore a mauve dress, vermilion-shot at the throat, and short enough to show the curved plumpness of her legs encased in fine unrumpled rose-tinted stockings. Her modish overcoat was lilac-gray lined with green and a large marine-blue rosette was bunched at the side of her neat gray hat.

In the Fifth Avenue shops she was waited upon as if she were a dark foreign lady of title visiting New York. In the afternoon she took a taxi-cab to Harlem.

Now all the fashionable people who called at Rose's house were generally her friends. And so Rose always went herself to let them in. She could look out from her window, one flight up, and ho-ho down to them.

When Madame Laura rang the bell, Rose popped her head out. Nobody I know, she thought, but the attractive woman in expensive clothes piqued her curiosity. Hastily she dabbed her face with powder pad, patted her hair into shape, and descended.

"Is Mr. Jacob Brown living here?" Madame Laura asked.

"Well, he was—I mean ——" This lux-

urious woman demanding Jake tantalized
Rose. She still referred to him as her man
since his disappearance. No reports of his
living with another woman having come to
her, she had told her friends that Jake's
mother had come between them.

"He always had a little some'n' of a mam-
ma's boy about him, you know."

Poor Jake. Since he left home, his mother
had become for him a loving memory only.
When you saw him, talked to him, he stood
forth as one of those unique types of humanity
who lived alone and were never lonely. You
would hardly wonder who were his father and
mother and what they were like. He, in his
frame and atmosphere, was the Alpha and
Omega himself.

"I mean— Can you tell me what you
want?" asked Rose.

"Must I? I didn't know he— Why,
he wrote to me. Said he was ill. And sent
his friend to tell me he was ill. Can't I see
him?"

"Did he write to you from this here address?"

"Why, certainly. I have his card here." Madame Laura was fumbling in her handbag.

A triumphant smile stole into Rose's face. Jake had no real home and had to use her address.

"Is you his sister or what?"

"I'm a friend," Madame Laura said, sharply.

"Well, he's got a nearve." Rose jerked herself angrily. "He's mah man."

"I didn't come all the way here to hear that," said Madame Laura. "I thought he was sick and wanting attention."

"Ain't I good enough to give him all the attention required without another woman come chasing after him?"

"Disgusting!" cried Madame Laura. "I would think this was a spohting house."

"Gwan with you before I spit in you' eye," cried Rose. "You look like some'n just outa one you'self."

"You're no lady," retorted Madame Laura, and she hurried down the steps.

Rose amplified the story exceedingly in telling it to her friends. "I slapped her face for insulting me," she said.

Billy Biasse heard of it from the boy dancer of the Congo. When Billy went again to see Jake, one of the patrons of his gaming joint went with him. It was that yellow youth, the same one that had first invited Zeddy over to Gin-head Susy's place. He was a prince of all the day joints and night holes of the Belt. All the shark players of Dixie Red's pool-room were proud of losing a game to him, and at the Congo the waiters danced around to catch his orders. For Yaller Prince, so they affectionately called him, was living easy and sweet. Three girls, they said, were engaged in the business of keeping him princely—one chocolate-to-the-bone, one teasing-brown, and one yellow. He was always well dressed in a fine nigger-brown or bottle-green suit, excessively creased, and spats.

Also he was happy-going and very generous. But there was something slimy about him.

Yaller Prince had always admired Jake, in the way a common-bred admires a thoroughbred, and hearing from Billy that he was ill, he had brought him fruit, cake, and ice cream and six packets of Camels. Yaller Prince was more intimate with Jake's world than Billy, who swerved off at a different angle and was always absorbed in the games and winnings of men.

Jake and Yaller had many loose threads to pick up again and follow for a while. Were the gin parties going on still at Susy's? What had become of Miss Curdy? Yaller didn't know. He had dropped Myrtle Avenue before Zeddy did.

"Susy was free with the gin all right, but, gee whizzard! She was sure black and ugly, buddy," remarked Yaller.

"You said it, boh," agreed Jake. "They was some pair all right, them two womens. Black and ugly is exactly Susy, and that there

[237]

other Curdy creachur all streaky yaller and ugly. I couldn't love them theah kind."

Yaller uttered a little goat laugh. "I kain't stand them ugly grannies, either. But sometimes they does pay high, buddy, and when the paying is good, I can always transfer mah mind."

"I couldn't foh no price, boh," said Jake. "Gimme a nice sweet-skin brown. I ain't got no time foh none o' you' ugly hard-hided dames."

Jake asked for Strawberry Lips. He was living in Harlem again and working longshore. Up in Yonkers Zeddy was endeavoring to overcome his passion for gambling and start housekeeping with a steady home-loving woman. He was beginning to realize that he was not big enough to carry two strong passions, each pulling him in opposite directions. Some day a grandson of his born in Harlem might easily cope with both passions, might even come to sacrifice woman to gambling. But Zeddy himself was too close to the savage swell of life.

Ray entered with a friend whom he introduced as James Grant. He was also a student working his way through college. But lacking funds to continue, he had left college to find a job. He was fourth waiter on Ray's diner, succeeding the timid boy from Georgia. As both chairs were in use, Grant sat on the edge of the bed and Ray tipped up Jake's suitcase. . . .

Conversation veered off to the railroad.

"I am getting sick of it," Ray said. "It's a crazy, clattering, nerve-shattering life. I think I'll fall down for good."

"Why, ef you quit, chappie, I'll nevah go back on that there white man's sweet chariot," said Jake.

"Whasmat?" asked Billy Biasse. "Kain't you git along on theah without him?"

"It's a whole lot the matter you can't understand, Billy. The white folks' railroad ain't like Lenox Avenue. You can tell on theah when a pal's a real pal."

"I got a pal, I got a gal," chanted Billy,

"heah in mah pocket-book." He patted his
breast pocket.

"Go long from here with you' lonesome
haht, you wolf," cried Jake.

"Wolf is mah middle name, but . . . I
ain't bad as I hear, and ain't you mah buddy,
too?" Billy said to Jake. "Git you'self going
quick and come on down to mah place, son.
The bones am lonesome foh you."

Billy and Yaller Prince left.

"Who is the swell strutter?" Ray's friend
asked.

"Hm! . . . I knowed him long time in
Harlem," said Jake. "He's a good guy. Just
brought me all them eats and cigarettes."

"What does he work at?" asked Ray.

"Nothing menial. He's a p-i." . . .

"Low-down yaller swine," said Ray's
friend. "Harlem is stinking with them."

"Oh, Yaller is all right, though," said Jake.
"A real good-hearted scout."

"Good-hearted!" Grant sneered. "A man's
heart is cold dead when he has women doing
that for him. How can a man live that way

and strut in public, instead of hiding himself underground like a worm?" He turned indignantly to Ray.

"Search me!" Ray laughed a little. "You might as well ask why all mulattoes have unpleasant voices."

Grant was slightly embarrassed. He was yellow-skinned and his voice was hard and grainy. Jake he-hawed.

"Not all, chappie, I know some with sweet voice."

"Mula*tress, mon ami.*" Ray lifted a finger. "That's an exception. And now, James, let us forget Jake's kind friend."

"Oh, I don't mind him talking," said Jake. "I don't approve of Yaller's trade mahself, but ef he can do it, well— It's because you don't know how many womens am running after the fellahs jest begging them to do that. They been after me moh time I can remember. There's lots o' folks living easy and living sweet, but . . ."

"There are as many forms of parasitism as there are ways of earning a living," said Ray.

"But to live the life of carrion," sneered Grant, "fatten on rotting human flesh. It's the last ditch, where dogs go to die. When you drop down in that you cease being human."

"You done said it straight out, brother," said Jake. "It's a stinking life and I don't like stinks."

"Your feeling against that sort of thing is fine, James," said Ray. "But that's the most I could say for it. It's all right to start out with nice theories from an advantageous point in life. But when you get a chance to learn life for yourself, it's quite another thing. The things you call fine human traits don't belong to any special class or nation or race of people. Nobody can pull that kind of talk now and get away with it, least of all a Negro."

"Why not?" asked Grant. "Can't a Negro have fine feelings about life?"

"Yes, but not the old false-fine feelings that used to be monopolized by educated and cultivated people. You should educate yourself away from that sort of thing."

"But education is something to make you fine!"

"No, modern education is planned to make you a sharp, snouty, rooting hog. A Negro getting it is an anachronism. We ought to get something new, we Negroes. But we get our education like—like our houses. When the whites move out, we move in and take possession of the old dead stuff. Dead stuff that this age has no use for."

"How's that?"

"Can you ask? You and I were born in the midst of the illness of this age and have lived through its agony. . . . Keep your fine feelings, indeed, but don't try to make a virtue of them. You'll lose them, then. They'll become all hollow inside, false and dry as civilization itself. And civilization is rotten. We are all rotten who are touched by it."

"I am not rotten," retorted Grant, "and I couldn't bring myself and my ideas down to the level of such filthy parasites."

"All men have the disease of pimps in their hearts," said Ray. "We can't be civilized and not. I have seen your high and mighty civilized people do things that some pimps would be ashamed of——"

"You said it, then, and most truly," cried Jake, who, lying on the bed, was intently following the dialogue.

"Do it in the name of civilization," continued Ray. "And I have been forced down to the level of pimps and found some of them more than human. One of them was so strange. . . . I never thought he could feel anything. Never thought he could do what he did. Something so strange and wonderful and awful, it just lifted me up out of my little straight thoughts into a big whirl where all of life seemed hopelessly tangled and colored without point or purpose."

"Tell us about it," said Grant.

"All right," said Ray. "I'll tell it."

XVII

*I*T WAS in the winter of 1916 when I first came to New York to hunt for a job. I was broke. I was afraid I would have to pawn my clothes, and it was dreadfully cold. I didn't even know the right way to go about looking for a job. I was always timid about that. For five weeks I had not paid my rent. I was worried, and Ma Lawton, my landlady, was also worried. She had her bills to meet. She was a good-hearted old woman from South Carolina. Her face was all wrinkled and sensitive like finely-carved mahogany.

Every bed-space in the flat was rented. I was living in the small hall bedroom. Ma Lawton asked me to give it up. There were four men sleeping in the front room; two in an old, chipped-enameled brass bed, one on a davenport, and the other in a folding chair. The old lady put a little canvas cot in that

[245]

same room, gave me a pillow and a heavy quilt, and said I should try and make myself comfortable there until I got work.

The cot was all right for me. Although I hate to share a room with another person and the fellows snoring disturbed my rest. Ma Lawton moved into the little room that I had had, and rented out hers—it was next to the front room—to a man and a woman.

The woman was above ordinary height, chocolate-colored. Her skin was smooth, too smooth, as if it had been pressed and fashioned out for ready sale like chocolate candy. Her hair was straightened out into an Indian Straight after the present style among Negro ladies. She had a mongoose sort of a mouth, with two top front teeth showing. She wore a long mink coat.

The man was darker than the woman. His face was longish, with the right cheek somewhat caved in. It was an interesting face, an attractive, salacious mouth, with the lower lip protruding. He wore a bottle-green peg-top suit, baggy at the hips. His coat hung loose from his shoulders and it was much longer than the prevailing style. He wore also a Mexican hat, and in his breast pocket he carried an Ingersoll watch attached to a heavy gold chain. His name was Jericho Jones, and they called him Jerco for short. And she was Miss Whicher—Rosalind Whicher.

Ma Lawton introduced me to them and said I was broke, and they were both awfully nice to me. They took me to a big feed of corned beef and cabbage at Burrell's on Fifth Avenue. They gave me a good appetizing drink of gin to commence with. And we had beer with the eats; not ordinary beer, either, but real Budweiser, right off the ice.

And as good luck sometimes comes pouring down like a shower, the next day Ma Lawton got me a job in the little free-lunch saloon right under her flat. It wasn't a paying job as far as money goes in New York, but I was glad to have it. I had charge of the free-lunch counter. You know the little dry crackers that go so well with beer, and the cheese and fish and the potato salad. And I served,

besides, spare-ribs and whole boiled potatoes
and corned beef and cabbage for those customers who could afford to pay for a lunch. I
got no wages at all, but I got my eats twice
a day. And I made a few tips, also. For
there were about six big black men with plenty
of money who used to eat lunch with us, specially for our spare-ribs and sweet potatoes.
Each one of them gave me a quarter. I made
enough to pay Ma Lawton for my canvas cot.

Strange enough, too, Jerco and Rosalind
took a liking to me. And sometimes they
came and ate lunch perched up there at the
counter, with Rosalind the only woman there,
all made up and rubbing her mink coat against
the men. And when they got through eating,
Jerco would toss a dollar bill at me.

We got very friendly, we three. Rosalind
would bring up squabs and canned stuff from
the German delicatessen in One Hundred and
Twenty-fifth Street, and sometimes they asked
me to dinner in their room and gave me good
liquor.

I thought I was pretty well fixed for such

a hard winter. All I had to do as extra work was keeping the saloon clean. . . .

One afternoon Jerco came into the saloon with a man who looked pretty near white. Of course, you never can tell for sure about a person's race in Harlem, nowadays, when there are so many high-yallers floating round —colored folks that would make Italian and Spanish people look like Negroes beside them. But I figured out from his way of talking and acting that the man with Jerco belonged to the white race. They went in through the family entrance into the back room, which was unusual, for the family room of a saloon, as you know, is only for women in the business and the men they bring in there with them. Real men don't sit in a saloon here as they do at home. I suppose it would be sissified. There's a bar for them to lean on and drink and joke as long as they feel like.

The boss of the saloon was a little fidgety about Jerco and his friend sitting there in the back. The boss was a short pumpkin-bellied brown man, a little bald off the forehead.

Twice he found something to attend to in the back room, although there was nothing at all there that wanted attending to. . . . I felt better, and the boss, too, I guess, when Rosalind came along and gave the family room its respectable American character. I served Rosalind a Martini cocktail extra dry, and afterward all three of them, Rosalind, Jerco, and their friend, went up to Ma Lawton's.

The two fellows that slept together were elevator operators in a department store, so they had their Sundays free. On the afternoon of the Sunday of the same week that the white-looking man had been in the saloon with Jerco, I went upstairs to change my old shoes—they'd got soaking wet behind the counter—and I found Ma Lawton talking to the two elevator fellows.

The boys had given Ma Lawton notice to quit. They said they couldn't sleep there comfortably together on account of the goings-on in Rosalind's room. The fellows were members of the Colored Y. M. C. A. and were queerly quiet and pious. One of them was studying to be a preacher. They were the sort of fellows that thought going to cabarets a sin, and that parlor socials were leading Harlem straight down to hell. They only went to church affairs themselves. They had been rooming with Ma Lawton for over a year. She called them her gentlemen lodgers.

Ma Lawton said to me: "Have you heard anything phony outa the next room, dear?"

"Why, no, Ma," I said, "nothing more unusual than you can hear all over Harlem. Besides, I work so late, I am dead tired when I turn in to bed, so I sleep heavy."

"Well, it's the truth I do like that there Jerco an' Rosaline," said Ma Lawton. "They did seem quiet as lambs, although they was always havin' company. But Ise got to speak to them, 'cause I doana wanta lose ma young mens. . . . But theyse a real nice-acting couple. Jerco him treats me like him was mah son. It's true that they doan work like all poah niggers, but they pays that rent down good and prompt ehvery week."

Jerco was always bringing in ice-cream and

cake or something for Ma Lawton. He had a
way about him, and everybody liked him. He
was a sympathetic type. He helped Ma Lawton move beds and commodes and he fixed her
clothes lines. I had heard somebody talking
about Jerco in the saloon, however, saying that
he could swing a mean fist when he got his
dander up, and that he had been mixed up in
more than one razor cut-up. He did have a
nasty long razor scar on the back of his right
hand.

The elevator fellows had never liked Rosalind and Jerco. The one who was studying to
preach Jesus said he felt pretty sure that they
were an ungodly-living couple. He said that
late one night he had pointed out their room
to a woman that looked white. He said the
woman looked suspicious. She was perfumed
and all powdered up and it appeared as if she
didn't belong among colored people.

"There's no sure telling white from high-
yaller these days," I said. "There are so many
swell-looking quadroons and octoroons of the
race."

But the other elevator fellow said that one day in the tenderloin section he had run up against Rosalind and Jerco together with a petty officer of marines. And that just put the lid on anything favorable that could be said about them.

But Ma Lawton said: "Well, Ise got to run mah flat right an' try mah utmost to please youall, but I ain't wanta dip mah nose too deep in a lodger's affairs."

Late that night, toward one o'clock, Jerco dropped in at the saloon and told me that Rosalind was feeling badly. She hadn't eaten a bite all day and he had come to get a pail of beer, because she had asked specially for draught beer. Jerco was worried, too.

"I hopes she don't get bad," he said. "For we ain't got a cent o' money. Wese just in on a streak o' bad luck."

"I guess she'll soon be all right," I said.

The next day after lunch I stole a little time and went up to see Rosalind. Ma Lawton was just going to attend to her when I let myself in, and she said to me: "Now the poor woman is sick, poor chile, ahm so glad mah conscience is free and that I hadn't a said nothing evil t' her."

Rosalind was pretty sick. Ma Lawton said it was the grippe. She gave Rosalind hot whisky drinks and hot milk, and she kept her feet warm with a hot-water bottle. Rosalind's legs were lead-heavy. She had a pain that pinched her side like a pair of pincers. And she cried out for thirst and begged for draught beer.

Ma Lawton said Rosalind ought to have a doctor. "You'd better go an' scares up a white one," she said to Jerco. "Ise nevah had no faith in these heah nigger doctors."

"I don't know how we'll make out without money," Jerco whined. He was sitting in the old Morris chair with his head heavy on his left hand.

"You kain pawn my coat," said Rosalind. "Old man Greenbaum will give you two hundred down without looking at it."

"I won't put a handk'chief o' yourn in the

hock shop," said Jerco. "You'll need you' stuff soon as you get better. Specially you' coat. You kain't go anywheres without it."

"S'posin' I don't get up again," Rosalind smiled. But her countenance changed suddenly as she held her side and moaned. Ma Lawton bent over and adjusted the pillows.

Jerco pawned his watch chain and his own overcoat, and called in a Jewish doctor from the upper Eighth Avenue fringe of the Belt. But Rosalind did not improve under medical treatment. She lay there with a sad, tired look, as if she didn't really care what happened to her. Her lower limbs were apparently paralyzed. Jerco told the doctor that she had been sick unto death like that before. The doctor shot a lot of stuff into her system. But Rosalind lay there heavy and fading like a felled tree.

The elevator operators looked in on her. The student one gave her a Bible with a little red ribbon marking the chapter in St. John's Gospel about the woman taken in adultery.

He also wanted to pray for her recovery. Jerco wanted the prayer, but Rosalind said no. Her refusal shocked Ma Lawton, who believed in God's word.

The doctor stopped Rosalind from drinking beer. But Jerco slipped it in to her when Ma Lawton was not around. He said he couldn't refuse it to her when beer was the only thing she cared for. He had an expensive sweater. He pawned it. He also pawned their large suitcase. It was real leather and worth a bit of money.

One afternoon Jerco sat alone in the back room of the saloon and began to cry.

"I'd do anything. There ain't anything too low I wouldn't do to raise a little money," he said.

"Why don't you hock Rosalind's fur coat?" I suggested. "That'll give you enough money for a while."

"Gawd, no! I wouldn't touch none o' Rosalind's clothes. I jest kain't," he said. "She'll need them as soon as she's better."

"Well, you might try and find some sort of a job, then," I said.

"Me find a job? What kain I do? I ain't no good foh no job. I kain't work. I don't know how to ask for no job. I wouldn't know how. I wish I was a woman."

"Good God! Jerco," I said, "I don't see any way out for you but some sort of a job."

"What kain I do? What kain I do?" he whined. "I kain't do nothing. That's why I don't wanta hock Rosalind's fur coat. She'll need it soon as she's better. Rosalind's so wise about picking up good money. Just like that!" He snapped his fingers.

I left Jerco sitting there and went into the saloon to serve a customer a plate of corned beef and cabbage.

After lunch I thought I'd go up to see how Rosalind was making out. The door was slightly open, so I slipped in without knocking. I saw Jerco kneeling down by the open wardrobe and kissing the toe of one of her brown shoes. He started as he saw me, and looked queer kneeling there. It was a high old-fashioned wardrobe that Ma Lawton must have picked up at some sale. Rosalind's coat was hanging there, and it gave me a spooky feeling, for it looked so much more like the real Rosalind than the woman that was dozing there on the bed.

Her other clothes were hanging there, too. There were three gowns—a black silk, a glossy green satin, and a flimsy chiffon-like yellow thing. In a corner of the lowest shelf was a bundle of soiled champagne-colored silk stockings and in the other four pairs of shoes—one black velvet, one white kid, and another gold-finished. Jerco regarded the lot with dog-like affection.

"I wouldn't touch not one of her things until she's better," he said. "I'd sooner hock the shirt off mah back."

Which he was preparing to do. He had three expensive striped silk shirts, presents from Rosalind. He had just taken two out of the wardrobe and the other off his back,

and made a parcel of them for old Greenbaum. . . . Rosalind woke up and murmured
that she wanted some beer. . . .

A little later Jerco came to the saloon with
the pail. He was shivering. His coat collar
was turned up and fastened with a safety pin,
for he only had an undershirt on.

"I don't know what I'd do if anything hap-
pens to Rosalind," he said. "I kain't live
without her."

"Oh yes, you can," I said in a not very sympathetic tone. Jerco gave me such a reproach-
ful pathetic look that I was sorry I said it.

The tall big fellow had turned into a
scared, trembling baby. "You ought to buck
up and hold yourself together," I told him.
"Why, you ought to be game if you like Rosalind, and don't let her know you're down in
the dumps."

"I'll try," he said. "She don't know how
miserable I am. When I hooks up with a
woman I treat her right, but I never let her
know everything about me. Rosalind is an

awful good woman. The straightest woman
I ever had, honest."

I gave him a big glass of strong whisky.

Ma Lawton came in the saloon about nine
o'clock that evening and said that Rosalind
was dead. "I told Jerco we'd have to sell that
theah coat to give the poah woman a decent
fun'ral, an' he jest brokes down crying like a
baby."

That night Ma Lawton slept in the kitchen
and put Jerco in her little hall bedroom. He
was all broken up. I took him up a pint of
whisky.

"I'll nevah find another one like Rosalind,"
he said, "nevah!" He sat on an old black-
framed chair in which a new yellow-var-
nished bottom had just been put. I put my
hand on his shoulder and tried to cheer him
up: "Buck up, old man. Never mind, you'll
find somebody else." He shook his head.
"Perhaps you didn't like the way me and
Rosalind was living. But she was one naturally good woman, all good inside her."

[260]

I felt foolish and uncomfortable. "I always liked Rosalind, Jerco," I said, "and you, too. You were both awfully good scouts to me. I have nothing against her. I am nothing myself."

Jerco held my hand and whimpered: "Thank you, old top. Youse all right. Youse always been a regular fellar."

It was late, after two a. m. I went to bed. And, as usual, I slept soundly.

Ma Lawton was an early riser. She made excellent coffee and she gave the two elevator runners and another lodger, a porter who worked on Ellis Island, coffee and hot home-made biscuits every morning. The next morning she shook me abruptly out of my sleep.

"Ahm scared to death. Thar's moah tur'ble trouble. I kain't git in the barfroom and the hallway's all messy."

I jumped up, hauled on my pants, and went to the bathroom. A sickening purplish liquid coming from under the door had trickled down the hall toward the kitchen. I took Ma

Lawton's rolling-pin and broke through the door.

Jerco had cut his throat and was lying against the bowl of the water-closet. Some empty coke papers were on the floor. And he sprawled there like a great black boar in a mess of blood.

A FAREWELL FEED

XVIII

RAY and Grant had found jobs on a freighter that was going down across the Pacific to Australia and from there to Europe. Ray had reached the point where going any further on the railroad was impossible. He had had enough to vomit up of Philadelphia and Baltimore, Pittsburgh and Washington. More than enough of the bar-to-bar camaraderie of railroad life.

And Agatha was acting wistfully. He knew what would be the inevitable outcome of meeting that subtle wistful yearning halfway. Soon he would become one of the contented hogs in the pigpen of Harlem, getting ready to litter little black piggies. If he could have felt about things as Jake, how different his life might have been! Just to hitch up for a short while and be irresponsible! But he and Agatha were slaves of the civilized tradition. . . .

[263]

Harlem nigger strutting his stuff. . . Harlem
niggers! How often he had listened to those
phrases, like jets of saliva, spewing from the
lips of his work pals. They pursued, scared,
and haunted him. He was afraid that some
day the urge of the flesh and the mind's han-
kering after the pattern of respectable comfort
might chase his high dreams out of him and
deflate him to the contented animal that was a
Harlem nigger strutting his stuff. "No happy-
nigger strut for me," he would mutter, when
the feeling for Agatha worked like a fever in
his flesh. He saw destiny working in her
large, dream-sad eyes, filling them with the
passive softness of resignation to life, and seeking to encompass and yoke him down as just
one of the thousand niggers of Harlem. And
he hated Agatha and, for escape, wrapped
himself darkly in self-love.

Oh, he was scared of that long red steel
cage whose rumbling rollers were eternally
heavy-lipped upon shining, continent-circling
rods. If he forced himself to stay longer he
would bang right off his head. Once upon a

time he used to wonder at that great body of people who worked in nice cages: bank clerks in steel-wire cages, others in wooden cages, salespeople behind counters, neat, dutiful, respectful, all of them. God! how could they carry it on from day to day and remain quietly obliging and sane? If the railroad had not been cacophonous and riotous enough to balance the dynamo roaring within him, he would have jumped it long ago.

Life burned in Ray perhaps more intensely than in Jake. Ray felt more and his range was wider and he could not be satisfied with the easy, simple things that sufficed for Jake. Sometimes he felt like a tree with roots in the soil and sap flowing out and whispering leaves drinking in the air. But he drank in more of life than he could distill into active animal living. Maybe that was why he felt he had to write.

He was a reservoir of that intense emotional energy so peculiar to his race. Life touched him emotionally in a thousand vivid ways. Maybe his own being was something of a touchstone of the general emotions of his race. Any upset—a terror-breathing, Negro-baiting headline in a metropolitan newspaper or the news of a human bonfire in Dixie—could make him miserable and despairingly despondent like an injured child. While any flash of beauty or wonder might lift him happier than a god. It was the simple, lovely touch of life that charmed and stirred him most. . . . The warm, rich-brown face of a Harlem girl seeking romance . . . a late wet night on Lenox Avenue, when all forms are soft-shadowy and the street gleams softly like a still, dim stream under the misted yellow lights. He remembered once the melancholy-comic notes of a "Blues" rising out of a Harlem basement before dawn. He was going to catch an early train and all that trip he was sweetly, deliciously happy humming the refrain and imagining what the interior of the little dark den he heard it in was like. "Blues" . . . melancholy-comic. That was the key to himself and to his race. That strange, child-like capacity for wistfulness-and-laughter. . . .

No wonder the whites, after five centuries of contact, could not understand his race. How could they when the instinct of comprehension had been cultivated out of them? No wonder they hated them, when out of their melancholy environment the blacks could create mad, contagious music and high laughter. . . .

Going away from Harlem. . . . Harlem! How terribly Ray could hate it sometimes. Its brutality, gang rowdyism, promiscuous thickness. Its hot desires. But, oh, the rich blood-red color of it! The warm accent of its composite voice, the fruitiness of its laughter, the trailing rhythm of its "blues" and the improvised surprises of its jazz. He had known happiness, too, in Harlem, joy that glowed gloriously upon him like the high-noon sunlight of his tropic island home.

How long would he be able to endure the life of a cabin boy or mess boy on a freighter? Jake had tried to dissuade him. "A seaman's life is no good, chappie, and it's easier to jump off a train in the field than offn a ship gwine across the pond."

"Maybe it's not so bad in the mess," suggested Ray.

" 'Deed it's worse foh mine, chappie. Stoking and A. B. S. is cleaner work than messing with raw meat and garbage. I never was in love with no kitchen job. And tha's why I ain't none crazy about the white man's chuchuing buggy."

Going away from Harlem. . . .

Jake invited Ray and Grant to a farewell feed, for which Billy Biasse was paying. Billy was a better pal for Jake than Zeddy. Jake was the only patron of his gambling house that Billy really chummed with. They made a good team. Their intimate interests never clashed. And it never once entered Jake's head that there was anything ugly about Billy's way of earning a living. Tales often came roundabout to Billy of patrons grumbling that "he was swindling poah hardworking niggers outa their wages." But he had never heard of Jake backbiting.

"The niggers am swindling themselves," Billy always retorted. "I runs a gambling place foh the gang and they pays becas they love to gamble. I plays even with them mahself. I ain't no miser hog like Nije Gridley."

Billy liked Jake because Jake played for the fun of the game and then quit. Gambling did not have a strangle hold upon him any more than dope or desire did. Jake took what he wanted of whatever he fancied and . . . kept going.

The feed was spread at Aunt Hattie's cookshop. Jake maintained that Aunt Hattie's was the best place for good eats in Harlem. A bottle of Scotch whisky was on the table and a bottle of gin.

While the boys sampled the fine cream tomato soup, Aunt Hattie bustled in and out of the kitchen, with a senile-fond look for Jake and an affectionate phrase, accompanied by a salacious lick of her tongue.

"Why, it's good and long sence you ain't been in reg'lar to see me, chile. Whar's you been keeping you'self?"

"Ain't been no reg'lar chile of Harlem sence I done jump on the white man's chu-chu," said Jake.

"And is you still on that theah business?" Aunt Hattie asked.

"I don't know ef I is and I don't know ef I ain't. Ise been laid off sick."

"Sick! Poah chile, and I nevah knowed so I could come off'ring you a li'l' chicken broth. You jest come heah and eats any time you wanta, whether youse got money or not."

Aunt Hattie shuffled back to the kitchen to pick the nicest piece of fried chicken for Jake.

"Always in luck, Jakey," said Billy. "It's no wonder you nevah see niggers in the bread line. And you'll nevah so long as theah's good black womens like Aunt Hattie in Harlem."

Jake poured Scotch for three.

"Gimme gin," said Billy.

Jake called to Aunt Hattie to bring her glass. "What you gwine to have, Auntie?"

"Same thing youse having, chile," replied Aunt Hattie.

"This heah stuff is from across the pond."

"Lemme taste it, then. Ef youse always so eye-filling drinking it, it might ginger up mah bones some."

"Well, here's to us, fellahs," cried Billy. "Let's hope that hard luck nevah turn our glasses down or shet the door of a saloon in our face."

Glasses clinked and Aunt Hattie touched Jake's twice and closed her eyes as with trembling hand she guzzled.

"You had better said, 'Le's hope that this heah Gawd's own don't shut the pub in our face'," replied Jake. "Prohibition is right under our tail."

Everybody laughed. . . . Ray bit into the tender leg of his fried chicken. The candied sweet potatoes were sweeter than honey to his palate.

"Drink up, fellahs," said Billy.

"Got to leave you, Harlem," Ray sang lightly. "Got to turn our backs on you."

"And our black moon on the Pennsy," added Jake.

"Tomorrow the big blue beautiful ocean," said Ray.

"You'll puke in it," Jake grinned devilishly. "Why not can the idea, chappie? The sea is hell and when you hits shore it's the same life all ovah."

"I guess you are right," replied Ray. "Goethe said the same thing in *Werther*."

"Who is that?" Jake asked.

"A German ———"

"A boche?"

"Yes, a great one who made books instead of war. He was mighty and contented like a huge tame elephant. Genteel lovers of literature call that Olympian."

Jake gripped Ray's shoulder: "Chappie, I wish I was edjucated mahself."

"Christ! What for?" demanded Ray.

"Becaz I likes you." Like a black Pan out of the woods Jake looked into Ray's eyes with frank savage affection and Billy Biasse exclaimed:

"Lawdy in heaben! A li'l' foreign booze gwine turn you all soft?"

"Can't you like me just as well as you are?" asked Ray. "I can't feel any difference at all. If I was famous as Jack Johnson and rich as Madame Walker I'd prefer to have you as my friend than—President Wilson."

"Like bumbole you would!" retorted Jake. "Ef I was edjucated, I could, understand things better and be proper-speaking like you is. . . . And I mighta helped mah li'l sister to get edjucated, too (she must be a li'l' woman, now), and she would be nice-speaking like you' sweet brown, good enough foh you to hitch up with. Then we could all settle down and make money like edjucated people do, instead a you gwine off to throw you'self away on some lousy dinghy and me chasing around all the time lak a hungry dawg."

"Oh, you heart-breaking, slobbering nigger!" cried Billy Biasse. "That's the stuff youse got tuck away there under your tough black hide."

"Muzzle you' mouf," retorted Jake. "Sure Ise human. I ain't no lonesome wolf lak you is."

"A wolf is all right ef he knows the jungle."

"The fact is, Jake," Ray said, "I don't know what I'll do with my little education. I wonder sometimes if I could get rid of it and go and lose myself in some savage culture in the jungles of Africa. I am a misfit—as the doctors who dole out newspaper advice to the well-fit might say—a misfit with my little education and constant dreaming, when I should be getting the nightmare habit to hog in a whole lot of dough like everybody else in this country. Would you like to be educated to be like me?"

"If I had your edjucation I wouldn't be slinging no hash on the white man's chu-chu," Jake responded.

"Nobody knows, Jake. Anyway, you're happier than I as you are. The more I learn the less I understand and love life. All the learning in this world can't answer this little question, Why are we living?"

"Why, becaz Gawd wants us to, chappie," said Billy Biasse.

"Come on le's all go to Uncle Doc's," said

Jake, "and finish the night with a li'l' sweet jazzing. This is you last night, chappie. Make the most of it, foh there ain't no jazzing like Harlem jazzing over the other side."

They went to Uncle Doc's, where they drank many ceremonious rounds. Later they went to Leroy's Cabaret. . . .

The next afternoon the freighter left with Ray signed on as a mess boy.

THIRD PART

XIX

*T*HE lovely trees of Seventh Avenue were a vivid flame-green. Children, lightly clad, skipped on the pavement. Light open coats prevailed and the smooth bare throats of brown girls were a token as charming as the first pussy-willows. Far and high over all, the sky was a grand blue benediction, and beneath it the wonderful air of New York tasted like fine dry champagne.

Jake loitered along Seventh Avenue. Crossing to Lenox, he lazied northward and over the One Hundred and Forty-ninth Street bridge into the near neighborhood of the Bronx. Here, just a step from compactly-built, teeming Harlem, were frame houses and open lots and people digging. A colored couple dawdled by, their arms fondly caressing each other's hips. A white man fork-

[279]

ing a bit of ground stopped and stared expressively after them.

Jake sat down upon a mound thick-covered with dandelions. They glittered in the sun away down to the rear of a rusty-gray shack. They filled all the green spaces. Oh, the common little things were glorious there under the sun in the tender spring grass. Oh, sweet to be alive in that sun beneath that sky! And to be in love—even for one hour of such rare hours! One day! One night! Somebody with spring charm, like a dandelion, seasonal and haunting like a lovely dream that never repeats itself. . . . There are hours, there are days, and nights whose sheer beauty overwhem us with happiness, that we seek to make even more beautiful by comparing them with rare human contacts. . . . It was a day like this we romped in the grass . . . a night as soft and intimate as this on which we forgot the world and ourselves. . . . Hours of pagan abandon, celebrating ourselves. . . .

And Jake felt as all men who love love for love's sake can feel. He thought of the surg-

ing of desire in his boy's body and of his
curious pure nectarine beginnings, without
pain, without disgust, down home in Virginia.
Of his adolescent breaking-through when the
fever-and-pain of passion gave him a wonderful strange-sweet taste of love that he had
never known again. Of rude contacts and
swift satisfactions in Norfolk, Baltimore, and
other coast ports. . . . Havre. . . . The
West India Dock districts of London. . . .

"Only that cute heart-breaking brown of the
Baltimore," he mused. "A day like this sure
feels like her. Didn't even get her name. O
Lawdy! what a night that theah night was.
Her and I could sure make a hallelujah picnic
outa a day like this." . . .

Jake and Billy Biasse, leaving Dixie Red's
pool-room together, shuffled into a big excited
ring of people at the angle of Fifth Avenue
and One Hundred and Thirty-third Street.
In the ring three bad actors were staging a
rough play—a yellow youth, a chocolate
youth, and a brown girl.

The girl had worked herself up to the highest pitch of obscene frenzy and was sicking the dark strutter on to the yellow with all the filthiest phrases at her command. The two fellows pranced round, menacing each other with comic gestures.

"Why, ef it ain't Yaller Prince!" said Jake.

"Him sure enough," responded Billy Biasse. "Guess him done laid off from that black gal why she's shooting her stinking mouth off at him."

"Is she one of his producing goods?"

"She was. But I heard she done beat up another gal of hisn—a fair-brown that useta hand over moh change than her and Yaller turn' her loose foh it." . . .

"You lowest-down face-artist!" the girl shrieked at Yaller Prince. "I'll bawl it out so all a Harlem kain know what you is." And ravished by the fact that she was humiliating her one-time lover, she gesticulated wildly.

"Hit him, Obadiah!" she yelled to the chocolate chap. "Hit him I tell you. Beat his mug up foh him, beat his mug and bleed his

mouf." Over and over again she yelled:
"Bleed his mouf!" As if that was the thing in
Yaller Prince she had desired most. For it
she had given herself up to the most unthink-
able acts of degradation. Nothing had been
impossible to do. And now she would cut and
bruise and bleed that mouth that had once
loved her so well so that he should not smile
upon her rivals for many a day.

"Two-faced yaller nigger, you does ebery
low-down thing, but you nevah done a lick of
work in you lifetime. Show him, Obadiah.
Beat his face and bleed his mouf."

"Yaller nigger," cried the extremely bandy-
legged and grim-faced Obadiah, "Ise gwine
kick you pants."

"I ain't scared a you, black buzzard," Yaller Prince replied in a thin, breathless voice,
and down he went on his back, no one knowing
whether he fell or was tripped up. Obadiah
lifted a bottle and swung it down upon his
opponent. Yaller Prince moaned and blood
bubbled from his nose and his mouth.

"He's a sweet-back, all right, but he ain't

a strong one," said some one in the crowd. The police had been conspicuously absent during the fracas, but now a baton tap-tapped upon the pavement and two of them hurried up. The crowd melted away.

Jake had pulled Yaller Prince against the wall and squatted to rest the bleeding head against his knee.

"What's matter here now? What's matter?" the first policeman, with revolver drawn, asked harshly.

"Nigger done beat this one up and gone away from heah, tha's whatsmat," said Billy Biasse.

They carried Yaller Prince into a drugstore for first aid, and the policeman telephoned for an ambulance. . . .

"We gotta look out foh him in hospital. He was a pretty good skate for a sweetman," Billy Biasse said.

"Poor Yaller!" Jake, shaking his head, commented; "it's a bad business."

"He's plumb crazy gwine around without a gun when he's a-playing that theah game," said Billy, "with all these cut-thwoat niggers in Harlem ready to carve up one another foh a li'l' insisnificant humpy."

"It's the same ole life everywhere," responded Jake. "In white man's town or nigger town. Same bloody-sweet life across the pond. I done lived through the same blood-battling foh womens ovah theah in London. Between white and white and between white and black. Done see it in the froggies' country, too. A mess o' fat-headed white soldiers them was knocked off by apaches. Don't tell *me* about cut-thwoat niggers in Harlem. The whole wul' is boody-crazy——"

"But Harlem is the craziest place foh that, I bet you, boh," Billy laughed richly. "The stuff it gives the niggers brain-fevah, so far as I see, and this heah wolf has got a big-long horeezon. Wese too thick together in Harlem. Wese all just lumped together without a chanst to choose and so we nacherally hate one another. It's nothing to wonder that you' buddy Ray done runned away from it. Why, jest the other night I witnessed a nasty stroke.

You know that spade prof that's always there on the Avenue handing out the big stuff about niggers and their rights and the wul' and bolschism. . . . He was passing by the pool-room with a bunch o' books when a bad nigger jest lunges out and socks him bif! in the jaw. The poah frightened prof. started picking up his books without a word said, so I ups and asks the boxer what was the meaning o' that pass. He laughed and asked me ef I really wanted to know, and before he could squint I landed him one in the eye and pulled mah gun on him. I chased him off that corner all right. I tell you, boh, Harlem is lousy with crazy-bad niggers, as tough as Hell's Kitchen, and I always travel with mah gun ready."

"And ef all the niggers did as you does," said Jake, "theah'd be a regular gun-toting army of us up here in the haht of the white man's city. . . . Guess ef a man stahts gunning after you and means to git you he will someways ———"

"But you might git him fierst, too, boh, ef youse in luck."

"I mean ef you don't know he's gunning after you," said Jake. "I don't carry no weapons nonetall, but mah two long hands."

"Youse a punk customer, then, I tell you," declared Billy Biasse, "and no real buddy o' mine. Ise got a A number one little barker I'll give it to you. You kain't lay you'self wide open lak thataways in this heah burg. No boh!"

Jake went home alone in a mood different from the lyrical feelings that had fevered his blood among the dandelions. "Niggers fixing to slice one another's throats. Always fighting. Got to fight if youse a man. It ain't because Yaller was a p-i. . . . It coulda been me or anybody else. Wese too close and thick in Harlem. Need some moh fresh air between us. . . . Hitting out at a edjucated nigger minding his own business and without a word said. . . . Guess Billy is right toting his silent dawg around with him. He's gotta, though, when he's running a gambling joint. All the same, I gambles mahself and you nevah know when niggers am gwineta git crazy-mad.

Guess I'll take the li'l' dawg offn Billy, all right. It ain't costing me nothing." . . .

In the late afternoon he lingered along Seventh Avenue in a new nigger-brown suit. The fine gray English suit was no longer serviceable for parade. The American suit did not fit him so well. Jake saw and felt it. . . . The only thing he liked better about the American suit was the pantaloons made to wear with a belt. And the two hip pockets. If you have the American habit of carrying your face-cloth on the hip instead of sticking it up in your breast pocket like a funny decoration, and if, like Billy Biasse, you're accustomed to toting some steely thing, what is handier than two hip pockets?

Except for that, Jake had learned to prefer the English cut of clothes. Such first-rate tweed stuff, and so cheap and durable compared with American clothes! Jake knew nothing of tariff laws and naïvely wondered why the English did not spread their fine cloth all over the American clothes market. . . . He worked up his shoulders in his nigger-brown coat. It didn't feel right, didn't hang so well. There was something a little too chic in American clothes. Not nearly as awful as French, though, Jake horse-laughed, vividly remembering the popular French styles. Broad-pleated, long-waisted, tight-bottomed pants and close-waisted coats whose breast pockets stick out their little comic signs of color. . . . Better color as a savage wears it, or none at all, instead of the Frenchman's peeking bit. The French must consider the average bantam male killing handsome, and so they make clothes to emphasize all the angular elevated rounded and pendulated parts of the anatomy. . . .

The broad pavements of Seventh Avenue were colorful with promenaders. Brown babies in white carriages pushed by little black brothers wearing nice sailor suits. All the various and varying pigmentation of the human race were assembled there: dim brown, clear brown, rich brown, chestnut, copper, yellow, near-white, mahogany, and gleaming anthracite. Charming brown matrons, proud

yellow matrons, dark nursemaids pulled a
zigzag course by their r e s t i v e little
charges. . . .

And the elegant strutters in faultless spats;
West Indians, carrying canes and wearing
trousers of a different pattern from their coats
and vests, drawing sharp comments from their
Afro-Yank rivals.

Jake mentally noted: "A dickty gang sure
as Harlem is black, but——"

The girls passed by in bright batches of
color, according to station and calling. High
class, menial class, and the big trading class,
flaunting a front of chiffon-soft colors framed
in light coats, seizing the fashion of the day to
stage a lovely leg show and spilling along the
Avenue the perfume of Djer-kiss, Fougère,
and Brown Skin.

"These heah New York gals kain most sar-
tainly wear some moh clothes," thought Jake,
"jest as nifty as them French gals." . . .

Twilight was enveloping the Belt, merging
its life into a soft blue-black symphony. . . .
The animation subsided into a moment's

pause, a muffled, tremulous soul-stealing note
. . . then electric lights flared everywhere,
flooding the scene with dazzling gold.

Jake went to Aunt Hattie's to feed. Billy
Biasse was there and a gang of longshoremen
who had boozed and fed and were boozing
again and, touched by the tender spring night,
were swapping love stories and singing:

"Back home in Dixie is a brown gal there,
   Back home in Dixie is a brown gal there,
   Back home in Dixie is a brown gal there,
      Back home in Dixie I was bawn in.

"Back home in Dixie is a gal I know,
   Back home in Dixie is a gal I know,
   Back home in Dixie is a gal I know,
      And I wonder what nigger is saying to her a bootiful
      good mawnin'."

A red-brown West Indian among them vol-
unteered to sing a Port-of-Spain song. It immortalized the drowning of a young black
sailor. It was made up by the bawdy colored
girls of the port, with whom the deceased had

been a favorite, and became very popular
among the stevedores and sailors of the island.

> "Ring the bell again,
> Ring the bell again,
> Ring the bell again,
> But the sharks won't puke him up.
> Oh, ring the bell again.
>
> "Empty is you' room,
> Empty is you' room,
> Empty is you' room,
> But you find one in the sea.
> Oh, empty is you' room.
>
> "Ring the bell again,
> Ring the bell again,
> Ring the bell again,
> But we know who feel the pain.
> Oh, ring the bell again."

The song was curious, like so many Negro
songs of its kind, for the strange strengthening
of its wistful melody by a happy rhythm that
was suitable for dancing.

Aunt Hattie, sitting on a low chair, was
swaying to the music and licking her lips, her

wrinkled features wearing an expression of ecstatic delight. Billy Biasse offered to stand a bottle of gin. Jake said he would also sing a sailor song he had picked up in Limehouse. And so he sang the chanty of Bullocky Bill who went up to town to see a fair young maiden. But he could not remember most of the words, therefore Bullocky Bill cannot be presented here. But Jake was boisterously applauded for the scraps of it that he rendered.

The singing finished, Jake confided to Billy: "I sure don't feel lak spending a lonesome night this heah mahvelous night."

"Ain't nobody evah lonely in Harlem that don't wanta be," retorted Billy. "Even yours truly lone Wolf ain't nevah lonesome."

"But I want something as mahvelous as mah feelings."

Billy laughed and fingered his kinks: "Harlem has got the right stuff, boh, for all feelings."

"Youse right enough," Jake agreed, and fell into a reverie of full brown mouth and mischievous brown eyes all composing a perfect whole for his dark-brown delight.

"You wanta take a turn down the Congo?" asked Billy.

"Ah no."

"Rose ain't there no moh."

Rose had stepped up a little higher in her profession and had been engaged to tour the West in a Negro company.

"All the same, I don't feel like the Congo tonight," said Jake. "Le's go to Sheba Palace and jazz around a little."

Sheba Palace was an immense hall that was entirely monopolized for the amusements of the common workaday Negroes of the Belt. Longshoremen, kitchen-workers, laundresses, and W. C. tenders—all gravitated to the Sheba Palace, while the upper class of servitors—bell-boys, butlers, some railroad workers and waiters, waitresses and maids of all sorts— patronized the Casino and those dancings that were given under the auspices of the churches.

The walls of Sheba Palace were painted

with garish gold, and tables and chairs were
screaming green. There were green benches
also lined round the vast dancing space. The
music stopped with an abrupt clash just as
Jake entered. Couples and groups were
drinking at tables. Deftly, quickly the waiters
slipped a way through the tables to serve and
collect the money before the next dance. . . .
Little white-filled glasses, little yellow-filled
glasses, general guzzling of gin and whisky.
Little saucy brown lips, rouged maroon, sucking up iced crème de menthe through straws,
and many were sipping the golden Virginia
Dare, in those days the favorite wine of the
Belt. On the green benches couples lounged,
sprawled, and, with the juicy love of spring
and the liquid of Bacchus mingled in fascinating white eyes curious in their dark frames,
apparently oblivious of everything outside of
themselves, were loving in every way but . . .

The orchestra was tuning up. . . . The
first notes fell out like a general clapping for
merrymaking and chased the dancers running,
sliding, shuffling, trotting to the floor. Little

girls energetically chewing Spearmint and
showing all their teeth dashed out on the floor
and started shivering amorously, itching for
their partners to come. Some lads were
quickly on their feet, grinning gayly and im-
provising new steps with snapping of fingers
while their girls were sucking up the last of
their crème de menthe. The floor was large
and smooth enough for anything.

They had a new song-and-dance at the
Sheba and the black fellows were playing it
with *éclat*.

> Brown gal crying on the corner,
> Yaller gal done stole her candy,
> Buy him spats and feed him cream,
> Keep him strutting fine and dandy.

> Tell me, pa-pa, Ise you' ma-ma,
> Yaller gal can't make you fall,
> For Ise got some loving pa-pa
> Yaller gal ain't got atall.

"Tell me, pa-pa, Ise you' ma-ma." The black
players grinned and swayed and let the music
go with all their might. The yellow in the
music must have stood out in their imagina-

tion like a challenge, conveying a sense of that primitive, ancient, eternal, inexplicable antagonism in the color taboo of sex and society. The dark dancers picked up the refrain and jazzed and shouted with delirious joy, "Tell me, pa-pa, Ise you' ma-ma." The handful of yellow dancers in the crowd were even more abandoned to the spirit of the song. "White," "green," or "red" in place of "yaller" might have likewise touched the same deep-sounding, primitive chord. . . .

> Yaller gal sure wants mah pa-pa,
>   But mah chocolate turns her down,
> 'Cause he knows there ain't no loving
>   Sweeter than his loving brown.

> Telli me, pa-pa, Ise you' ma-ma,
>   Yaller gal can't make you fall,
> For Ise got some loving pa-pa
>   Yaller gal ain't got atall.

Jake was doing his dog with a tall, shapely quadroon girl when, glancing up at the balcony, he spied the little brown that he had entirely given over as lost. She was sitting at a table while "Tell me pa-pa" was tickling

[297]

everybody to the uncontrollable point—she was sitting with her legs crossed and well exposed, and, with the aid of the mirror attached to her vanity case, was saucily and nonchalantly powdering her nose.

The quadroon girl nearly fell as Jake, without a word of explanation, dropped her in the midst of a long slide and, dashing across the floor, bounded up the stairs.

"Hello, sweetness! What youse doing here?"

The girl started and knocked over a glass of whisky on the floor: "O my Gawd! it's mah heartbreaking daddy! Where was you all this time?"

Jake drew a chair up beside her, but she jumped up: "Lawdy, no! Le's get outa here quick, 'cause Ise got somebody with me and now I don't want see him no moh."

"'Sawright, I kain take care of mahself," said Jake.

"Oh, honey, no! I don't want no trouble and he's a bad actor, that nigger. See, I done break his glass o' whisky and tha's bad luck.

[298]

Him's just theah in the lav'try. Come quick. I don't want him to ketch us."

And the flustered little brown heart hustled Jake down the stairs and out of the Sheba Palace.

"Tell me, pa-pa, Ise you' ma-ma . . ."

The black shouting chorus pursued them outside.

"There ain't no yaller gal gwine get mah honey daddy thisanight." She took Jake's arm and cuddled up against his side.

"Aw no, sweetness. I was dogging it with one and jest drops her flat when I seen you."

"And there ain't no nigger in the wul' I wouldn't ditch foh you, daddy. O Lawdy! How Ise been crazy longing to meet you again."

XX

"*W*HAR'S we gwine?" Jake asked.

They had walked down Madison Avenue, turned on One Hundred and Thirtieth Street, passing the solid gray-grim mass of the whites' Presbyterian church, and were under the timidly whispering trees of the decorously silent and distinguished Block Beautiful. . . . The whites had not evacuated that block yet. The black invasion was threatening it from One Hundred and Thirty-first Street, from Fifth Avenue, even from behind in One Hundred and Twenty-ninth Street. But desperate, frightened, blanch-faced, the ancient sepulchral Respectability held on. And giving them moral courage, the Presbyterian church frowned on the corner like a fortress against the invasion. The Block Beautiful was worth a struggle. With its charming green lawns and quaint white-fronted houses, it preserved

[300]

the most Arcadian atmosphere in all New York. When there was a flat to let in that block, you would have to rubber-neck terribly before you saw in the corner of a window-pane a neat little sign worded, Vacancy. But groups of loud-laughing-and-acting black swains and their sweethearts had started in using the block for their afternoon promenade. That was the limit: the desecrating of that atmosphere by black love in the very shadow of the gray, gaunt Protestant church! The Ancient Respectability was getting ready to flee. . . .

The beautiful block was fast asleep. Up in the branches the little elfin green things were barely whispering. The Protestant church was softened to a shadow. The atmosphere was perfect, the moment sweet for something sacred.

The burning little brownskin cuddled up against Jake's warm tall person: "Kiss me, daddy," she said. He folded her closely to him and caressed her. . . .

"But whar was you all this tur'bly long time?" demanded Jake.

Light-heartedly, she frisky like a kitten, they sauntered along Seventh Avenue, far from the rough environment of Sheba Palace.

"Why, daddy, I waited foh you all that day after you went away and all that night! Oh, I had a heart-break on foh you, I was so tur'bly disappointed. I nev' been so crazy yet about no man. Why didn't you come back, honey?"

Jake felt foolish, remembering why. He said that shortly after leaving her he had discovered the money and the note. He had met some of his buddies of his company who had plenty of money, and they all went celebrating until that night, and by then he had forgotten the street.

"Mah poor daddy!"

"Even you' name, sweetness, I didn't know. Ise Jake Brown—Jake for ev'body. What is you', sweetness?"

"They calls me Felice."

"Felice. . . . But I didn't fohget the cabaret nonatall. And I was back theah hunting foh you that very night and many moh after, but I nevah finds you. Where was you?"

"Why, honey, I don't lives in cabarets all mah nights 'cause Ise got to work. Furthermore, I done went away that next week to Palm Beach——"

"Palm Beach! What foh?"

"Work of course. What you think? You done brokes mah heart in one mahvelous night and neveh returns foh moh. And I was jest right down sick and tiahd of Harlem. So I went away to work. I always work. . . . I know what youse thinking, honey, but I ain't in the reg'lar business. 'Cause Ise a funny gal. I kain't go with a fellah ef I don't like him some. And ef he kain make me like him enough I won't take nothing off him and ef he kain make me fall the real way, I guess I'd work like a wop for him."

"Youse the baby I been waiting foh all along," said Jake. "I knowed you was the goods."

"Where is we gwine, daddy?"

"Ise got a swell room, sweetness, up in

'Fortiet' Street whar all them dickty shines
live."

"But kain you take me there?"

"Sure thing, baby. Ain't no nigger renting
a room in Harlem whar he kain't have his li'l'
company."

"Oh, goody, goody, honey-stick!"

Jake took Felice home to his room. She
was delighted with it. It was neat and orderly.

"Your landlady must be one of them proper
persons," she remarked. "How did you find
such a nice place way up here?"

"A chappie named Ray got it foh me when
I was sick ——"

"O Lawdy! was it serious? Did they all
take good care a you?"

"It wasn't nothing much and the fellahs was
all awful good spohts, especially Ray."

"Who is this heah Ray?"

Jake told her. She smoothed out the
counterpane on the bed, making a mental note
that it was just right for two. She admired
the geraniums in the window that looked on
the large court.

"These heah new homes foh niggers am **sure** nice," she commented.

She looked behind the curtain where his clothes were hanging and remarked his old English suit. Then she regarded archly his new nigger-brown rig-out.

"You was moh illegant in that other, but I likes you in this all the same."

Jake laughed. "Everything's gotta wear out some day."

Felice hung round his neck, twiddling her pretty legs.

He held her as you might hold a child and she ruffled his thick mat of hair and buried her face in it. She wriggled down with a little scream:

"Oh, I gotta go get mah bag!"

"I'll come along with you," said Jake.

"No, lemme go alone. I kain manage better by mahself."

"But suppose that nigger is waiting theah foh you? You better lemme come along."

"No, honey, I done figure he's waiting still in Sheba Palace, or boozing. Him and some

[305]

friends was all drinking befoh and he was kinder full. Ise sure he ain't gone home. Anyway, I kain manage by mahself all right, but ef you comes along and we runs into him— No, honey, you stays right here. I don't want messing up in no blood-baff. Theah's too much a that in Harlem."

They compromised, Felice agreeing that Jake should accompany her to the corner of Seventh Avenue and One Hundred and Thirty-fifth Street and wait for her there. She had not the faintest twinge of conscience herself. She had met the male that she preferred and gone with him, leaving the one that she was merely makeshifting with. It was a very simple and natural thing to her. There was nothing mean about it. She was too nice to be mean. However, she was aware that in her world women scratched and bit into each other's flesh and men razored and gunned at each other over such things. . . .

Felice recalled one memorable afternoon when two West Indian women went for each other in the back yard of a house in One Hundred and Thirty-second Street. One was a laundress, a whopping brown woman who had come to New York from Colon, and the other was a country girl, a buxom Negress from Jamaica. They were quarreling over a vain black bantam, one of the breed that delight in women's scratching over them. The laundress had sent for him to come over from the Canal Zone to New York. They had lived together there and she had kept him, making money in all the ways that a gay and easy woman can on the Canal Zone. But now the laundress bemoaned the fact that "sence mah man come to New Yawk, him jest gone back on me in the queerest way you can imagine."

Her man, in turn, blamed the situation upon her, said she was too aggressive and mannish and had harried the energy out of him. But the other girl seemed to endow him again with virility. . . . After keeping him in Panama and bringing him to New York, the laundress hesitated about turning her male loose in Harlem, although he was apparently of no more value to her. But his rejuvenating

experience with the younger girl had infuri-
ated the laundress. A sister worker from
Alabama, to whom she had confided her secret
tragedy, had hinted: "Lawdy! sistah, that sure
sounds phony-like. Mebbe you' man is jest
playing 'possum with you." And the laundress was crazy with suspicion and jealousy
and a feeling for revenge. She challenged her
rival to fight the affair out. They were all
living in the same house. . . .

Felice also lived in that house. And one
afternoon she was startled by another girl
from an adjoining room pounding on her
door and shrieking: "Open foh the love of
Jesus! . . . Theah's sweet hell playing in the
back yard."

The girls rushed to the window and saw the
two black women squaring off at each other
down in the back yard. They were stark
naked.

After the challenge, the women had decided
to fight with their clothes off. An old custom,
perhaps a survival of African tribalism, had
been imported from some remote West Indian

hillside into a New York back yard. Perhaps, the laundress had thought, that with her heavy and powerful limbs she could easily get her rival down and sit on her, mauling her properly. But the black girl was as nimble as a wild goat. She dodged away from the laundress who was trying to get ahold of her big bush of hair, and suddenly sailing fullfront into her, she seized the laundress, shoulder and neck, and butted her twice on the forehead as only a rough West Indian country girl can butt. The laundress staggered backward, groggy, into a bundle of old carpets. But she rallied and came back at the grinning Negress again. The laundress had never learned the brutal art of butting. The girl bounded up at her forehead with another well-aimed butt and sent her reeling flop on her back among the carpets. The girl planted her knees upon the laundress's high chest and wrung her hair.

"You don't know me, but I'll make you remember me foreber. I'll beat you' mug ugly. There!" Bam! Bam! She slapped the laundress's face.

"Git off mah stomach, nigger gal, and leave me in peace," the laundress panted. The entire lodging-house was in a sweet fever over the event. Those lodgers whose windows gave on the street had crowded into their neighbors' rear rooms and some had descended into the basement for a close-up view. Apprised of the naked exhibtion, the landlord hurried in from the corner saloon and threatened the combatants with the police. But there was nothing to do. The affair was settled and the women had already put their shifts on.

The women lodgers cackled gayly over the novel staging of the fight.

"It sure is better to disrobe like that, befoh battling," one declared. "It turn you' hands and laigs loose for action."

"And saves you' clothes being ripped into ribbons," said another.

A hen-fight was more fun than a cock-fight, thought Felice, as she hastily threw her things into her bag. The hens pluck feathers, but they never wring necks like the cocks.

[310]

And Jake. Standing on the corner, he waited, restive, nervous. But, unlike Felice, his thought was not touched by the faintest fear of a blood battle. His mind was a circle containing the girl and himself only, making a thousand plans of the joys they would create together. She was a prize to hold. Had slipped through his fingers once, but he wasn't ever going to lose her again. That little model of warm brown flesh. Each human body has its own peculiar rhythm, shallow or deep or profound. Transient rhythms that touch and pass you, unrememberable, and rhythms unforgetable. Imperial rhythms whose vivid splendor blinds your sight and destroys your taste for lesser ones.

Jake possessed a sure instinct for the right rhythm. He was connoisseur enough. But although he had tasted such a varied many, he was not raw animal enough to be undiscriminating, nor civilized enough to be cynical. . . .

Felice came hurrying as much as she could along One Hundred and Thirty-fifth Street,

bumping a cumbersome portmanteau on the
pavement and holding up one unruly lemon-
bright silk stocking with her left hand. Jake
took the bag from her. They went into a
delicatessen store and bought a small cold
chicken, ham, mustard, olives, and bread.
They stopped in a sweet shop and bought a
box of chocolate-and-vanilla ice-cream and
cake. Felice also took a box of chocolate
candy. Their last halt was at a United Cigar
Store, where Jake stocked his pockets with a
half a dozen packets of Camels. . . .

Felice had just slipped out of her charming
strawberry frock when her hands flew down to
her pretty brown leg. "O Gawd! I done fohget something!" she cried in a tone that inti-
mated something very precious.

"What's it then?" demanded Jake.

"It's mah luck," she said. "It's the fierst
thing that was gived to me when I was born.
Mah gran'ma gived it and I wears it always
foh good luck."

This lucky charm was an old plaited necklace, leathery in appearance, with a large,

antique blue bead attached to it, that Felice's
grandmother (who had superintended her
coming into the world) had given to her immediately after that event. Her grandmother
had dipped the necklace into the first water
that Felice was washed in. Felice had reli-
giously worn her charm around her neck all
during her childhood. But since she was
grown to ripe girlhood and low-cut frocks
were the fashion and she loved them so much,
she had transferred the unsightly necklace
from her throat to her leg. But before going
to the Sheba Palace she had unhooked the
thing. And she had forgotten it there in the
closet, hanging by a little nail against the
wash-bowl.

"I gotta go get it," she said.

"Aw no, you won't bother," drawled Jake.
And he drew the little agitated brown body to
him and quieted it. "It was good luck you
fohget it, sweetness, for it made us find one
another."

"Something to that, daddy," Felice said,
and her mouth touched his mouth.

[313]

They wove an atmosphere of dreams around them and were lost in it for a week. Felice asked the landlady to let her use the kitchen to cook their meals at home. They loitered over the wide field and lay in the sweet grass of Van Cortlandt Park. They went to the Negro Picture Theater and held each other's hand, gazing in raptures at the crude pictures. It was odd that all these cinematic pictures about the blacks were a broad burlesque of their home and love life. These colored screen actors were all dressed up in expensive evening clothes, with automobiles, and menials, to imitate white society people. They laughed at themselves in such rôles and the laughter was good on the screen. They pranced and grinned like good-nigger servants, who know that "mas'r" and "missus," intent on being amused, are watching their antics from an upper window. It was quite a little funny and the audience enjoyed it. Maybe that was the stuff the Black Belt wanted.

THE GIFT THAT BILLY GAVE

XXI

"*W*E GOTTA celebrate to-night," said Felice when Saturday came round again. Jake agreed to do anything she wanted. Monday they would have to think of working. He wanted to dine at Aunt Hattie's, but Felice preferred a "niftier" place. So they dined at the Nile Queen restaurant on Seventh Avenue. After dinner they subwayed down to Broadway. They bought tickets for the nigger heaven of a theater, whence they watched high-class people make luxurious love on the screen. They enjoyed the exhibition. There is no better angle from which one can look down on a motion picture than that of the nigger heaven.

They returned to Harlem after the show in a mood to celebrate until morning. Should they go to Sheba Palace where chance had been so good to them, or to a cabaret? Senti-

ment was in favor of Sheba Palace but her
love of the chic and novel inclined Felice
toward an attractive new Jewish-owned
Negro cabaret. She had never been there and
could not go under happier circumstances.

The cabaret was a challenge to any other in
Harlem. There were one or two cabarets in
the Belt that were distinguished for their im-
polite attitude toward the average Negro
customer, who could not afford to swill expensive drinks. He was pushed off into a corner
and neglected, while the best seats and service
were reserved for notorious little gangs of
white champagne-guzzlers from downtown.

The new cabaret specialized in winning the
good will of the average blacks and the approval of the fashionable set of the Belt. The
owner had obtained a college-bred Negro to
be manager, and the cashier was a genteel mulatto girl. On the opening night the manage-
ment had sent out special invitations to the
high lights of the Negro theatrical world and
free champagne had been served to them. The
new cabaret was also drawing nightly a crowd

of white pleasure-seekers from downtown.
The war was just ended and people were hungry for any amusements that were different
from the stale stock things.

Besides its spacious floor, ladies' room, gentlemen's room and coat-room, the new cabaret
had a bar with stools, where men could get together away from their women for a quick
drink and a little stag conversation. The bar
was a paying innovation. The old-line cabarets were falling back before their formidable
rival. . . .

The fashionable Belt was enjoying itself
there on this night. The press, theatrical, and
music world were represented. Madame
Mulberry was there wearing peacock blue
with patches of yellow. Madame Mulberry was a famous black beauty in the
days when Fifty-third Street was the hub of
fashionable Negro life. They called her then,
Brown Glory. She was the wife of Dick
Mulberry, a promoter of Negro shows. She
had no talent for the stage herself, but she
knew all the celebrated stage people of her

race. She always gossiped reminiscently of Bert Williams, George Walker and Aida Overton Walker, Anita Patti Brown and Cole and Johnson.

With Madame Mulberry sat Maunie Whitewing with a dapper cocoa-brown youth by her side, who was very much pleased by his own person and the high circle to which it gained him admission. Maunie was married to a nationally-known Negro artist, who lived simply and quietly. But Maunie was notorious among the scandal sets of Brooklyn, New York, and Washington. She was always creating scandals wherever she went, gallivanting around with improper persons at improper places, such as this new cabaret. Maunie's beauty was Egyptian in its exoticism and she dared to do things in the manner of ancient courtesans. Dignified colored matrons frowned upon her ways, but they had to invite her to their homes, nevertheless, when they asked her husband. But Maunie seldom went.

The sports editor of *Colored Life* was also there, with a prominent Negro pianist. It was rumored that Bert Williams might drop in after midnight. Madame Mulberry was certain he would.

James Reese Europe, the famous master of jazz, was among a group of white admirers. He had just returned from France, full of honors, with his celebrated band. New York had acclaimed him and America was ready to applaud. . . . That was his last appearance in a Harlem cabaret before his heart was shot out during a performance in Boston by a savage buck of his race. . . .

Prohibition was on the threshold of the country and drinking was becoming a luxury, but all the joy-pacers of the Belt who adore the novel and the fashionable and had a dollar to burn had come together in a body to fill the new cabaret.

The owner of the cabaret knew that Negro people, like his people, love the pageantry of life, the expensive, the fine, the striking, the showy, the trumpet, the blare—sumptuous settings and luxurious surroundings. And so he had assembled his guests under an enchanting-

blue ceiling of brilliant chandeliers and a
dome of artificial roses bowered among green
leaves. Great mirrors reflected the variegated
colors and poses. Shaded, multi-colored side-
lights glowed softly along the golden walls.

It was a scene of blazing color. Soft, barbaric, burning, savage, clashing, planless colors—all rioting together in wonderful harmony. There is no human sight so rich as an
assembly of Negroes ranging from lacquer
black through brown to cream, decked out in
their ceremonial finery. Negroes are like
trees. They wear all colors naturally. And
Felice, rouged to a ravishing maroon, and
wearing a close-fitting, chrome-orange frock
and cork-brown slippers, just melted into the
scene.

They were dancing as Felice entered and
she led Jake right along into it.

"Tell me, pa-pa, Ise you ma-ma . . ."

Every cabaret and dancing-hall was playing
it. It was the tune for the season. It had car-

ried over from winter into spring and was still the favorite. Oh, ma-ma! Oh, pa-pa!

The dancing stopped. . . . A brief interval and a dwarfish, shiny black man wearing a red-brown suit, with kinks straightened and severely plastered down in the Afro-American manner, walked into the center of the floor and began singing. He had a massive mouth, which he opened wide, and a profoundly big and quite good voice came out of it.

"I'm so doggone fed up, I don't know what to do.
  Can't find a pal that's constant, can't find a gal that's
    true.
  But I ain't gwine to worry 'cause mah buddy was a ham;
  Ain't gwine to cut mah throat 'cause mah gal ain't worf
    a damn.
  Ise got the blues all ovah, the coal-black biting blues,
  Like a prowling tom-cat that's got the low-down mews.

'I'm gwine to lay me in a good supply a gin,
  Foh gunning is a crime, but drinking ain't no sin.
  I won't do a crazy deed 'cause of a two-faced pal,
  Ain't gwineta break mah heart ovah a no-'count gal
  Ise got the blues all ovah, the coal-black biting blues,
  Like a prowling tom-cat that's got the low-down mews."

There was something of the melancholy

charm of Tschaikovsky in the melody. The black singer made much of the triumphant note of strength that reigned over the sad motif. When he sang, "I ain't gwine to cut mah throat," "Ain't gwine to break mah heart," his face became grim and full of will as a bull-dog's.

He conquered his audience and at the finish he was greeted with warm applause and a shower of silver coins ringing on the tiled pavement. An enthusiastic white man waved a dollar note at the singer and, to show that Negroes could do just as good or better, Maunie Whitewing's sleek escort imitated the gesture with a two-dollar note. That started off the singer again.

> "Ain't gwine to cut mah throat . . .
> Ain't gwine to break mah heart . . ."

"That zigaboo is a singing fool," remarked Jake.

Billy Biasse entered resplendent in a new bottle-green suit, and joined Jake and Felice at their table.

"What you say, Billy?" Jake's greeting.

"I say Ise gwineta blow. Toss off that theah liquor, you two. Ise gwineta blow champagne as mah compliments, old top." . . .

"Heah's good luck t'you, boh, and plenty of joy-stuff and happiness," continued Billy, when the champagne was poured. "You sure been hugging it close this week."

Jake smiled and looked foolish. . . . The second cook, whom he had not seen since he quitted the railroad, entered the cabaret with a mulatto girl on his arm and looked round for seats. Jake stood up and beckoned him over to his table.

"It's awright, ain't it Billy?" he asked his friend.

"Sure. Any friend a yourn is awright."

The two girls began talking fashion around the most striking dresses in the place. Jake asked about the demoted rhinoceros. He was still on the railroad, the second cook said, taking orders from another chef, "jest as savage and mean as ever, but not so moufy. I hear you friend Ray done quit us for the ocean, Jakey." . . .

There was still champagne to spare, nevertheless the second cook invited the boys to go up to the bar for a stiff drink of real liquor.

Negroes, like all good Americans, love a bar. I should have said, Negroes under Anglo-Saxon civilization. A bar has a charm all of its own that makes drinking there pleasanter. We like to lean up against it, with a foot on the rail. We will leave our women companions and choice wines at the table to snatch a moment of exclusive sex solidarity over a thimble of gin at the bar.

The boys left the girls to the fashions for a little while. Billy Biasse, being a stag as always, had accepted the invitation with alacrity. He loved to indulge in naked man-stuff talk, which would be too raw even for Felice's ears. As they went out Maunie Whitewing (she was a traveled woman of the world and had been abroad several times with and without her husband) smiled upon Jake with a bold stare and remarked to Madame

Mulberry: *"Quel beau garçon! J'aimerais beaucoup faire l'amour avec lui."*

"Superb!" agreed Madame Mulberry, appreciating Jake through her lorgnette.

Felice caught Maunie Whitewing's carnal stare at her man and said to the mulatto girl: "Jest look at that high-class hussy!"

And the dapper escort tried to be obviously unconcerned.

At the bar the three pals had finished one round and the bar-man was in the act of pouring another when a loud scream tore through music and conversation. Jake knew that voice and dashed down the stairs. What he saw held him rooted at the foot of the stairs for a moment. Zeddy had Felice's wrists in a hard grip and she was trying to wrench herself away.

"Leggo a me, I say," she bawled.

"I ain't gwineta do no sich thing. Youse mah woman."

"You lie! I ain't and you ain't mah man, black nigger."

"We'll see ef I ain't. Youse gwine home wif me right now."

Jake strode up to Zeddy. "Turn that girl loose."

"Whose gwineta make me?" growled Zeddy.

"I is. She's mah woman. I knowed her long before you. For Gawd's sake quit you' fooling and don't let's bust up the man's cabaret."

All the fashionable folk had already fled.

"She's *my* woman and I'll carve any damn-fool nigger for her." Lightning-quick Zeddy released the girl and moved upon Jake like a terrible bear with open razor.

"Don't let him kill him, foh Gawd's sake don't," a woman shrieked, and there was a general stampede for the exit.

But Zeddy had stopped like a cowed brute in his tracks, for leveled straight at his heart was the gift that Billy gave.

"Drop that razor and git you' hands up," Jake commanded, "and don't make a fool move or youse a dead nigger."

Zeddy obeyed. Jake searched him and found nothing. "I gotta good mind fixing you tonight, so you won't evah pull a razor on another man."

Zeddy looked Jake steadily in the face and said: "You kain kill me, nigger, ef you wanta. You come gunning at me, but you didn't go gunning after the Germans. Nosah! You was scared and runned away from the army."

Jake looked bewildered, sick. He was hurt now to his heart and he was dumb. The waiters and a few rough customers that the gun did not frighten away looked strangely at him.

"Yes, mah boy," continued Zeddy, "that's what life is everytime. When youse good to a buddy, he steals you woman and pulls a gun on you. Tha's what I get for prohceeding a slacker. A-llll right, boh, I was a good sucker, but—I ain't got no reason to worry sence youse down in the white folks' books." And he ambled away.

Jake shuffled off by himself. Billy Biasse tried to say a decent word, but he waved him away.

These miserable cock-fights, beastly, tiger-
ish, bloody. They had always sickened, sad-
dened, unmanned him. The wild, shrieking
mad woman that is sex seemed jeering at him.
Why should love create terror? Love should
be joy lifting man out of the humdrum ways
of life. He had always managed to delight in
love and yet steer clear of the hate and violence that govern it in his world. His love
nature was generous and warm without any
vestige of the diabolical or sadistic.

Yet here he was caught in the thing that he
despised so thoroughly. . . . Brest, London,
and his America. Their vivid brutality tor-
tured his imagination. Oh, he was infinitely
disgusted with himself to think that he had
just been moved by the same savage emotions
as those vile, vicious, villainous white men
who, like hyenas and rattlers, had fought,
murdered, and clawed the entrails out of black
men over the common, commercial flesh of
women. . . .

He reached home and sat brooding in the
shadow upon the stoop.

"Zeddy. My own friend in some ways. Naturally lied about me and the army, though. Playing martyr. How in hell did *he* get hooked up with her? Thought he was up in Yonkers. Would never guess one in a hundred it was he. What a crazy world! He must have passed us drinking at the bar. Wish I'd seen him. Would have had him drinking with us. And maybe we would have avoided that stinking row. Maybe and maybe not. Can't tell about Zeddy. He was always a bad-acting razor-flashing nigger."

A little hand timidly took his arm.

"Honey, you ain't mad at you sweetness, is you?"

"No. . . . I'm jest sick and tiah'd a everything."

"I nevah know you knowed one anether, honey. Oh, I was so scared. . . . But how could I know?"

"No, you couldn't. I ain't blaming nothing on you. I nevah would guess it was him mahself. I ain't blaming nobody at all."

Felice cuddled closer to Jake and fondled

his face. "It was a good thing you had you' gun, though, honey, or —— O Lawd! what mighta happened!"

"Oh, I woulda been a dead nigger this time or a helpless one," Jake laughed and hugged her closer to him. "It was Billy gived me that gun and I didn't even wanta take it."

"Didn't you? Billy is a good friend, eh?"

"You bet he is. Nevah gets mixed up with —in scraps like that."

"Honest, honey, I nevah liked Zeddy, but ——"

"Oh, you don't have to explain me nothing. I know it's jest connexidence. It coulda been anybody else. That don't worry mah skin."

"I really didn't like him, though, honey. Lemme tell you. I was kinder sorry for him. It was jest when I got back from Palm Beach I seen him one night at a buffet flat. And he was that nice to me. He paid drinks for the whole houseful a people and all because a me. I couldn't act mean, so I had to be nice mahself. And the next day he ups and buys me two pair a shoes and silk stockings and a box a chocolate candy. So I jest stayed on and gived him a li'l' loving, honey, but I nevah did tuk him to mah haht."

"It's awright, sweetness. What do I care so long as wese got one another again?"

She drew down his head and sought his mouth. . . .

"But what is we gwineta do, daddy? Sence they say that youse a slacker or deserter, I don't which is which ——"

"He done lied about that, though," Jake said, angrily. "I didn't run away because I was scared a them Germans. But I beat it away from Brest because they wouldn't give us a chance at them, but kept us in that rainy, sloppy, Gawd-forsaken burg working like wops. They didn't seem to want us niggers foh no soldiers. We was jest a bunch a despised hod-carriers, and Zeddy know that."

Now it was Felice's turn. "You ain't telling me a thing, daddy. I'll be slack with you and desert with you. What right have niggers got to shoot down a whole lot a Germans for? Is they worse than Americans or any other nation a white people? You done do the right thing, honey, and Ise with you and I love you the more for that. . . . But all the same, we can't stay in Harlem no longer, for the bulls will sure get you."

"I been thinking a gitting away from the stinking mess and go on off to sea again."

"Ah no, daddy," Felice tightened her hold on his arm. "And what'll become a me? I kain't go 'board a ship with you and I needs you."

Jake said nothing.

"What you wanta go knocking around them foreign countries again for like swallow come and swallow go from year to year and nevah settling down no place? This heah is you' country, daddy. What you gwine away from it for?"

"And what kain I do?"

"Do? Jest le's beat it away from Harlem, daddy. This heah country is good and big enough for us to git lost in. You know Chicago?"

"Haven't made that theah burg yet."

[332]

"Why, le's go to Chicago, then. I hear it's a mahvelous place foh niggers. Chicago, honey."

"When?"

"This heah very night. Ise ready. Ain't nothing in Harlem holding *me,* honey. Come on. Le's pack."

Zeddy rose like an apparition out of the shadow. Automatically Jake's hand went to his pocket.

"Don't shoot!" Zeddy threw up his hands. "I ain't here foh no trouble. I jest wanta ast you' pahdon, Jake. Excuse me, boh. I was crazy-mad and didn't know what I was saying. Ahm bloody well ashamed a mahself. But you know how it is when a gal done make a fool outa yóu. I done think it ovah and said to mah inner man: Why, you fool fellah, whasmat with you? Ef Zeddy slit his buddy's thwoat for a gal, that won't give back the gal to Zeddy. . . . So I jest had to come and tell it to you and ast you pahdon. You kain stay in Harlem as long as you wanta. Zeddy ain'ta gwineta open his mouf against you. You was always a good man-to-man buddy and nevah did wears you face ·bahind you. Don't pay no mind to what I done said in that theah cabaret. Them niggers hanging around was all drunk and wouldn't shoot their mouf off about you nohow. You ain't no moh slacker than me. What you done was all right, Jakey, and I woulda did it mahself ef I'd a had the guts to."

"It's all right, Zeddy," said Jake. "It was jest a crazy mix-up we all got into. I don't bear you no grudge."

"Will you take the paw on it?"

"Sure!" Jake gripped Zeddy's hand.

"So long, buddy, and fohgit it."

"So long, Zeddy, ole top." And Zeddy bear-walked off, without a word or a look at Felice, out of Jake's life forever. Felice was pleased, yet, naturally, just a little piqued. He might have said good-by to *me*, too, she thought. I would even have kissed him for the last time. She took hold of Jake's hands and swung them meditatively: "It's all right daddy, but——"

[334]

"But what?"

"I think we had better let Harlem miss us foh a little while."

"Scared?"

"Yes, daddy, but for you only. Zeddy won't go back on you. I guess not. But news is like a traveling agent, honey, going from person to person. I wouldn't take no chances."

"I guess youse right, sweetness. Come on, le's get our stuff together."

The two leather cases were set together against the wall. Felice sat upon the bed dangling her feet and humming "Tell me, pa-pa, Ise you ma-ma." Jake, in white shirt-sleeves, was arranging in the mirror a pink-yellow-and-blue necktie.

"ALL set! What you say, sweetness?"

"I say, honey, le's go to the Baltimore and finish the night and ketch the first train in the morning."

"Why, the Baltimore is padlocked!" said Jake.

"It was, daddy, but it's open again and go-

[335]

ing strong. White folks can't padlock niggers outa joy forever. Let's go, daddy."

She jumped down from the bed and jazzed
around.

"Oh, I nearly made a present of these heah
things to the landlady!" She swept from the
bed a pink coverlet edged with lace, and pil-
low-slips of the same fantasy (they were her
own make), with which she had replaced the
flat, rooming-house-white ones, and carefully
folded them to fit in the bag that Jake had
ready open for her. He slid into his coat,
made certain of his pocket-book, and picked
up the two bags.

The Baltimore was packed with happy,
grinning wrigglers. Many pleasure-seekers
who had left the new cabaret, on account of
the Jake-Zeddy incident, had gone there. It
was brighter than before the raid. The ceiling and walls were kalsomined in white and
lilac and the lights glared stronger from new
chandeliers.

The same jolly, compact manager was there,
grinning a welcome to strange white visitors,

who were pleased and never guessed what cautious reserve lurked under that grin.

Tell me, pa-pa, Ise you' ma-ma. . . .

Jake and Felice squeezed a way in among the jazzers. They were all drawn together in one united mass, wriggling around to the same primitive, voluptuous rhythm.

Tell me, pa-pa, Ise you' ma-ma. . . .

Haunting rhythm, mingling of naïve wistfulness and charming gayety, now sheering over into mad riotous joy, now, like a jungle mask, strange, unfamiliar, disturbing, now plunging headlong into the far, dim depths of profundity and rising out as suddenly with a simple, childish grin. And the white visitors laugh. They see the grin only. Here are none of the well-patterned, well-made emotions of the respectable world. A laugh might finish in a sob. A moan end in hilarity. That gorilla type wriggling there with his hands so strangely hugging his mate, may strangle her tonight. But he has no thought of that now. He loves the warm wriggle and is lost in it.

[337]

Simple, raw emotions and real. They may frighten and repel refined souls, because they are too intensely real, just as a simple savage stands dismayed before nice emotions that he instantly perceives are false.

Tell me, pa-pa, Ise you' ma-ma. . . .

Jake was the only guest left in the Baltimore. The last wriggle was played. The waiters were picking up things and settling accounts.

"Whar's the little hussy?" irritated and perplexed, Jake wondered.

Felice was not in the cabaret nor outside on the pavement. Jake could not understand how she had vanished from his side.

"Maybe she was making a high sign when you was asleep," a waiter laughed.

"Sleep hell!" retorted Jake. He was in no joking mood.

"We gwineta lock up now, big boy," the manager said.

Jake picked up the bags and went out on the sidewalk again. "I kain't believe she'd

ditch me like that at the last moment," he said
aloud. "Anyhow, I'm bound foh Chicago. I
done made up mah mind to go all becausing a
her, and I ain'ta gwineta change it whether she
throws me down or not. But sure she kain'ta
run off and leaves her suitcase. What the hell
is I gwine do with it?"

Felice came running up to him, panting,
from Lenox Avenue.

"Where in hell you been all this while?" he
growled.

"Oh, daddy, don't get mad!"

"Whar you been I say?"

"I done been to look for mah good-luck
necklace. I couldn't go to Chicago without
it."

Jake grinned. "Whyn't you tell me you
was gwine? Weren't you scared a Zeddy?"

"I was and I wasn't. Ef I'd a told you, you
woulda said it wasn't worth troubling about.
So I jest made up mah mind to slip off and git
it. The door wasn't locked and Zeddy wasn't
home. It was hanging same place where I
left it and I slipped it on mah leg and left the

keys on the table. You know I had the keys.
Ah, daddy, ef I'd a had mah luck with me, we
nevah woulda gotten into a fight at that
cabaret."

"You really think so, sweetness?"

They were walking to the subway station
along Lenox Avenue.

"I ain't thinking, honey. I knows it. I'll
nevah fohgit it again and it'll always give us
good luck."

THE END